Mystery at Monrovia Castle

THE REBECCA ORANGE CASTLE COZY MYSTERY SERIES
BOOK ONE

VALERIE BRANDY

EMERALD LION PRESS

Published by: Emerald Lion Press. 23901 Calabasas Rd., Ste 2088, Calabasas, CA 91302. emeraldlionpress@gmail.com

ISBN: 978-1-964161-59-4

Cover design by Mariah Sinclair. Editing provided by Sharon Lennon-Mehlschau.

Printed in the United States of America. To request permission to use passages from this book in any context other than a review, please contact the publisher at emeraldlionpress@gmail.com.

Visit the author's website at: www.valeriebrandy.com

🌸 Created with Vellum

Contents

CHAPTER
One

HAVE you ever been broken up with while cleaning the anal glands of a pygmy marmoset? I have. And let me tell you— it's humiliating. All animal trainers know that marmosets are the "mean girls" of any zoo. And I'm *sure* the one who saw me get dumped by my long-time boyfriend went straight back to her monkey friends and laughed behind my back for the rest of the day.

You haven't really hit a low point in life until you've been laughed at by a bunch of animals that throw their own poop around. At fifty-three years old, I've experienced some hard days in my life. But the memory of the day I got dumped in front of a monkey will haunt me forever. I'm thinking about it even now— three weeks later— as I nurse my second (okay, *third*) glass of wine while checking my emails in search of any response from the dozens of job applications I've filled out.

Oh yeah, that's the other thing I lost that day. My job.

In one swoop, a single moment destroyed my career, my relationship, and my dignity. But I'm not going to let that stop me. *This is an opportunity, Rebecca,* I keep telling myself. *An opportunity to start over on a brand new adventure.*

There's a padding sound as my constant companion, Joe,

lands at my feet near the end of the couch. He's a two-hundred-and-fifty pound Tibetan Mastiff, a breed that's usually reserved for monks that live in the mountains of Tibet, where they're ferocious protectors of castle-like monasteries. The only reason he came to me is he flunked basic training due to lack of aggression mixed with a lazy demeanor, and they needed someone willing to take a floofball with a stubborn streak. I named him Joe because he reminded me of my mechanic at the time. A little lazy. Unwilling to compromise. And not a mean bone in his body. I like to joke that even the Tibetan monks— known for their endless patience— couldn't handle Joe's lazy streak. He needed an animal trainer to turn him around. We were meant for each other.

He lays on my legs. His golden fur is a plush relief, but the weight of his enormous behind pushes me into the couch so hard I can barely breathe. If my laptop weren't on my lap, Joe would definitely try to cover my entire body with his. He's a dog that doesn't know his own heft. He looks over his shoulder at me, tongue out, a big smile on his face.

"That's perfect buddy," I tell him. "The crushing weight of your backside helps a lot, thank you." He tilts his head at me, his smile getting bigger. Joe has wide, empathetic eyes that are so human it's clear he knows how I'm feeling. He's been worried about me since the dumping happened. He can tell I'm in distress.

On that note, let me back up to the day of the dumping. It was an ordinary one as far as my life was concerned. Every day for the past twenty years, I'd gone to work at San Diego Safari Park, which is a haven for exotic animals. Our zoo is unlike any other in that the animals roam free across the exhibits, just like they would in the wild. Safari Trucks offer visitors an escape into the lands owned by animals, weaving past elephants, giraffes, and even lions, running across acres of open land instead of cooped up in cages. Visiting our park is as close as you can get to going on an African Safari without having to endure a fourteen hour flight.

I started working at the park fresh out of my master's program in zoology and remained there for decades. As a behaviorist and animal expert, I was responsible for teaching these exotic creatures behaviors (or, what some people call "tricks"), that made it possible for us to offer them the best care. I taught giraffes to turn in a circle not just because it was cute, but because it allowed us to better orient them for well-ness checks. I taught lions to lay down not just because it was a fun demonstration for visitors, but because it helped us when we needed to clean their teeth.

Basically, I had the best job in the world. And then— I met Travis.

Travis was charming in that dangerous kind of way. He was handsome and he knew it. He had dark hair that fell over his sea-glass eyes with a carefree ease. And he shared the same passion for animals that I did. We met when I was in my thirties, and I fell hard. The Safari Park hired him to head up the reptile unit, and seeing him every day meant my crush only grew. He never made a move so eventually I asked him out (a decision I very much regret, now).

The years slipped by and we were always boyfriend and girlfriend, but the ring never came. And I was fine with that, because— hey, nature is nature! Marriage is something human beings designed. You don't see penguins insisting on a piece of paper. They just love each other because it's natural.

At least, that's what I told myself.

Travis advanced in the department and eventually became *my* boss, which— looking back— bothers me a lot more now than it did when we were dating. I told myself his success was my success, but actually— it should have been *me* getting promoted to the head of the trainer program.

And then— the moment came.

We were in one of our many exam rooms, performing a

routine health check on one of our Pygmy Marmosets—Gypsy. Pygmy Marmosets are the Earth's smallest primates, and Gypsy was about the length of my ring finger. I was wearing rubber gloves, leaning over to try and express her delicate anal glands. Travis was by my side, and plexiglass windows in front of us allowed curious patrons to get an inside look at the care we offer our animals. That day, there was a huge crowd gathered. A little kid with a balloon. A dad with an ice-cream cone. Dozens of people stared at me as I cautiously flipped Gypsy over to look at her bum.

"Careful not to apply to much pressure," Travis said, tapping his hands on the table.

"You think this is my first set of anal glands?" I laughed. "Do you even *know* me?"

There was a long pause as Travis took in what I said. I glanced away from Gypsy, looking up into his ocean eyes. They were watering. Was he... *crying?*

"I *don't* know you," Travis said, wiping his face. "And that's my fault. Our relationship just happened and I let it happen but I never invested— not the way you deserve—"

I blinked at him. Gypsy flipped in my hand, looking up at us like we were the latest episode of her favorite soap opera.

"Travis—" I said, my heart pounding in my chest. "What did you do?"

"I cheated on you," he said. "More than once." He held up his hands as if to clarify. "With the same person!"

"Well, that's a relief," I had to strain to keep from shouting at him. "I believe that's what they call an *affair!*"

Gasps echoed from the crowd outside the window. I'd forgotten they could hear through the display. Murmurs rang throughout the group of tourists.

"Okay, I deserve that!" Travis answered. "I just couldn't keep it secret anymore and I had to tell you."

"And you thought *now* would be the perfect time?" I

motioned at the monkey in my hand and the crowd outside the plexiglass. The room spun. I had to know everything.

"Who is she?" I said, dreading the answer.

"Stacey," he admitted, referencing our dog sitter. The one who watched Joe when we were out of town. Apparently, she'd also learned how to walk and feed Travis.

"You've been sleeping with our dog sitter?!"

"She wants a job here," Travis said. "And I've told her I'd have to let you know first. So that it isn't— difficult."

"Difficult?" I said, and now I was shouting. "I've given you twenty years of my life and you want *Stacey* to date you and work here and—" then it hit me. "You're breaking up with me." The words sat heavy in the air. "We're done, aren't we? Just like that?"

There was a camera flash from behind the plexiglass. Someone in the crowd had taken a photo of the moment. I could only pray I wouldn't end up an internet meme. I glanced down at Gypsy, who looked at me with knowing eyes. It was as if she was saying, *Girl, I could have told you this would happen.* It was ironic that Gypsy was the one getting her anal glands expressed in front of a crowd, and even *she* was embarrassed for me.

And that's how I ended up here. Single. Looking for a job. I got to keep my condo at least, because it was purchased in my name before we even met. There were boxes already packed when I got home that evening. Travis couldn't move out fast enough, and— according to his Facebook posts— went straight to live with Stacey. I never thought at fifty I'd be starting over. But I'm not a quitter. I know there's new adventures on the horizon for me, if I can only be brave enough to take them.

As if timed by the universe, a dinging sound emanates from my email inbox. My pulse quickens.

A response from one of my job applications.

I click on it, reading as quickly as my eyes allow. It's a

phone interview offer from the *Offices of the Royal Family of Monrovia*. I remember the job posting well— it said they were looking for an animal expert to take care of the menagerie of animals that roam the castle grounds.

I glance down at Joe, still sitting heavy on my legs.

"Well, bud," I ask him. "Could you see us living in a castle?"

He lifts his head as if to say he couldn't picture himself living anywhere else. And if it's good enough for Joe, it's good enough for me. Still, a castle? Am I really in the headspace to pick up and move to another country I'd never even been to?

"Don't get too excited," I tell Joe, running my hands through his thick fur, which makes him roll over on his back. As he moves, the old Ikea couch we're sitting on groans because of his size. "It's just an interview. I'm only taking the call for practice. There's no way we're moving to a castle."

CHAPTER
Two

OH MY GOD, *I'm moving to a castle.*

The idea finally feels real as I pull an enormous suitcase through the airport, Joe's leash in one hand and my bag in another.

The phone interview felt like it was meant to be. We'd had the call just one week ago and I'd spoken to Maggie, the Royal Family's head of household assistant. "I handle everything pertaining to the grounds," she'd said over the phone, her voice light and easy. "From the rose gardens to the interior decorating to making sure the meals the kitchen is producing are up to standard— that's me!"

She explained that the Royal Family owned multiple properties across Monrovia, and that this particular castle was run by the nephew to the King and Queen, the Duke of Atwood. "They recently gave him the estate to manage, and his first concern was for the animals," Maggie said. "Many of them are legacy animals descended from ones kept by an Earl back in the Victorian era. We've done the best we can with them, but the Duke wants everything to be perfect. We need an expert. We need *you*," Maggie said, certainty in her voice.

"I'm really flattered," I offered, unable to believe this was happening. "But I'm not sure about moving to a new country. I won't even know the language."

Maggie snorted. "Monrovia was a British colony for years until there was a movement for independence. Everyone here still speaks English. You'll be fine! You'll fit right in. Think of it as a smaller Ireland, or Scotland..."

As she spoke, I opened up my computer and Googled Monrovia's location. It sat just near Croatia, and seemed to have a sea coast. The culture and language were influenced by the British, French, and Italian, becoming a melting pot after years of explorers stopped by the coast. I clicked on images and found pictures of quaint cobblestone towns with bright, pastel-colored buildings. Little coffee-shops offered al fresco dining. Rolling green hillsides beckoned. I couldn't help but imagine Joe roaming the open hills, chasing sheep, able to run free with no fences or end in sight.

"It looks like a dream," I said out-loud.

"It *is*," Maggie agreed. "And wait until you hear what the job pays..."

When she offered me the number, the words tumbled out of my mouth of their own accord. "I'm packing!"

Next thing I knew, we were arranging travel plans. Maggie took care of every detail, sending me frequent emails throughout the week with flight information, airport transfers, and meal preference requests. She also sent me pictures of my lodgings and asked for anything special Joe might need. It was clear Maggie was good at her job.

This must be how the other half lives, I thought as I answered yet another email from Maggie asking for a list of my favorite foods to keep in the fridge.

Now, standing in front of the VIP section of the airport check-in, I realize: I was right.

Maggie has booked me a first-class ticket, and even purchased a second seat for Joe to stretch out. We stand in front of a set of double doors marked *AIR-FRANCE VIP ONLY.* Joe looks at me as if he's not sure we belong here.

"Just act fancy, bud," I tell him, and I swear he straightens up his shoulders. We waltz toward a man standing outside the doors and present him with our tickets.

"We're flying first class," I say, the words feeling like they belong to someone else.

"Miss..." The man looks at the ticket. "Rebecca Orange?"

"That's me," I try to sound confident, but my voice comes out a little higher-pitched than usual.

"You're not flying first class," he answers.

My heart sinks. I knew this whole thing was too good to be true. I've probably been sucked into an internet scam. Maybe they're going to human traffic me. Best case scenario, the job is real but they're going to treat me like Cinderella, shoving me into some small servant's quarters and feeding me gruel.

"Oh," I say, deflated. "That's fine. I'll just head back to coach—"

I start to pull on Joe's leash but the man stops me. "You're flying first class *plus*," he says, nodding. "Our most premium offering."

"There's a first class *plus*?" I ask, my mouth dropping open.

"Of course, Miss Orange," he says, pointing at a single golden door off to the side. "Just through there. I can have someone escort you if you'd like. We have private butlers available for our premium customers..."

"No, that's fine," I say, staring at the golden door like it's Willy Wonka's Chocolate Factory. "We can find our own way."

I whistle at Joe and he falls into step behind me. Together, we push open that golden door and our new lives officially begin.

CHAPTER

Three

THE FIRST CLASS Plus waiting area is like nothing I've experienced in an airport. Couches coated in lush burgundy fabric create sitting spaces across the room. A table offers towers of different pastries, caviar, fancy cheeses, and crackers. A fridge with a see-through glass door lets guests choose drinks of every kind, on the house: sodas, wine, sparking water, kombucha. In the corner, a beauty attendant stands next to a collection of treatments for weary travelers, including face masks, moisturizers, and foot massages.

The only strange thing about the waiting area is that it's virtually empty. As far as customers go, there's only Joe, me, and one other man sitting across the room.

"Must be too expensive for most people, huh Joe?" I whisper in my dog's ear. He nods like he agrees with me. It's lonely at the top.

Out of curiosity, we glance at the only other VIP passenger. He's in his late forties— younger than me, but somewhat worse for wear. Wrinkles have formed around his eyes, and his hair is a dark salt and pepper grey. He's fit, though, and I can just make out the cover of the book he's reading. The title is in looping cursive and says, "*The Sociological Intersection of Politics and Daily Life.*"

I try to smile at him, but he's so engrossed in his book that it's like Joe and I don't exist. To keep myself entertained, I settle for feeding Joe crackers and cheese in exchange for practicing some of his behaviors. He runs through them all. He sits. He offers me a paw. I make a fake gun with my fingers and pretend to shoot it at him— Joe very convincingly plays dead.

An attendant comes to usher us down an attached walkway that leads to the plane, handling our luggage for us. In no time at all, we find our seats and take off. Once we reach cruising altitude, the lights go off, and everyone on the plane prepares to sleep.

"I could get used to this," I say to Joe, who's stretched out beside me.

I'm clothed in a silk pajama set, robe, and slippers, courtesy of the attendant who helped me change before we boarded. The chairs in First Class Plus are more like beds. We have our own contained little cabin, and a makeshift wall separates our two loungers from the rest of the plane. My seat lays flat so I can stretch out entirely, and I think this might be the first time I'll ever be able to sleep on a plane in my life. There's a TV in our private section, and I've chosen to put on *Bridget Jones's Diary.* Nothing like a good rom-com to start my new life.

A pang rises in my chest. *My new life.* Making this move means it's really over between Travis and me. I already knew it was over, of course, but something about taking off for a whole new country makes it real.

I'm still thinking about Travis when I look beside me, and realize one horrible fact: Joe is gone. Mere seconds ago he was resting by my side, but now, he's disappeared.

Great work, Rebecca, I think. *Only you could manage to lose sight of the world's biggest dog.*

I peek my head out from the top of the divider that keeps our little cocoon separate from the rest of the plane. *"Joe—"* I hiss. A whistle escapes my lips, which is usually his sign to return to me. But he doesn't come. "Joe!" I call a little louder.

My feet squish into the soft fabric of my slippers as I step out of my seat, pushing on the divider to exit our section. I walk across the aisle past a few similar private cabins, seeking any sign of Joe. And then: I see it.

His enormous golden tail, sticking out of the entrance to someone else's cocoon. It's wagging side-to-side, which can only mean trouble.

"Joe!" I hiss, walking straight for the cocoon and peering in the entrance. The man we saw in the VIP lounge is there, his book now closed beside him. His meal table is extended and there's an enormous plate of food in front of him. A glass of orange juice. Eggs. Bread. Jam. And... bacon.

Joe whips his head around, staring at me like he knows he's been caught. An entire strip of bacon hangs out of his mouth.

"I see you made a friend," I say to him, looking back at the man. I recognize him as the only other guest present in the VIP lounge.

"I couldn't resist," the man shrugs. His accent is hard to place. It's somewhere between British and Scottish, with round vowels and a little roll when he uses the letter "R."

"Joe has that effect on people," I shake my head. "Did he at least sit when you gave him the bacon?"

"Not once," the man laughs. "In fact, he tried to jump up in my lap. Are you depriving this dog of affection?"

"Hardly," I tell him. "He's a bottomless pit of need. No amount of snuggles are ever enough."

The man laughs and his eyes crinkle in the most charming way. He looked worse for wear in the VIP lounge, but I realize now that he may have just been tired from extended travel. After a short nap and some good food, he's actually quite handsome.

"I'm Rebecca," I say, holding out my hand. He shakes it.

"Jack," he answers. "I'm enjoying my last bit of your, what do you call it—" he pauses, thinking, "American breakfast? We don't have this in Monrovia."

"You don't have breakfast?!" I say, horrified.

"We do, but not *this*," He holds up a piece of bacon. "A side of ham perhaps but not this wonderful crispy invention you clever Americans have thought of."

"Joe's 'gonna miss that too, then," I pat Joe's back. "Is Monrovia a nice place to live?"

"I love it," he sighs. "It's unlike anywhere else. Are you moving there?"

"I guess we are," I shrug, still coming to terms with the idea. "We're moving to a place we've never even been. Is that crazy?" I lean forward on the arm rest of the chair. "It's kind of crazy isn't it?"

"Maybe it's just the start of a new adventure," Jack answers. "What's life without a bit of risk?" He smiles at me and there's something hypnotizing about it. "Perhaps, now that you're a new citizen of Monrovia, we'll run into each other again sometime and I can show you what the country has to offer. And Joe, of course."

Is he flirting with me? The idea seems impossible. I've had eyes for no one but Travis for so long, I'm not even sure what flirting is anymore. I'm struck by the urge to run away. But I settle for polite encouragement.

"I would like that," I answer. "Joe thanks you in advance."

"My pleasure," the man says. He passes me a piece of bacon and I lure Joe back into our private cocoon.

Joe settles back into his bed and I lay down beside him, placing a pillow under my head and resisting the urge to peek back over our dividing wall at Jack's cocoon. As I lay down on the lounger and stretch my legs out, *Bridget Jones' Diary* is still playing on the TV screen.

I'm going to an entirely new continent filled with men who aren't Travis. But some piece of me still misses my old life. Can I really start again in a new place? I roll over, putting an arm over Joe and thinking about everything I left behind, even though new possibilities wait just around the corner.

Why is letting go so hard?

CHAPTER
Four

THE FLIGHT GOES by in the blink of an eye. The few times I've crossed the Atlantic, it's been a tortuous experience marked by muscle aches, bad food, and minutes that click by like hours. But this flight? I was so comfortable and well-taken care of that time flew past. Now, I'm stretching my arms wide and rolling over on my lay-flat seat as the plane taxis its way to the private landing area. My eyes shift to Joe, as they so often do in the morning. He's the first creature I see when I wake up, and the first being I think of when the sun rises. He rolls over to face me, his tongue hanging out of his mouth, a big smile on his face.

I could get used to this, he seems to be saying. I pull him close and snuggle the top of his head, resting my face in his big, fluffy ears.

An attendant in a blue and white uniform comes to assist me in retrieving my luggage from the overhead compartment. And by "assist" I mean he does all the work for me. I just stand there stupidly as he pulls my enormous suitcases down.

"Are you sure I can't help?" I ask him, unable to relax. I'm a person who is used to taking care of her own things.

"Non!" the man exclaims. "Absolutely not, madame. You are our guest."

He assembles my luggage in a neat pile, strapping my carry-on tote to the handle of one of my suitcases. As he organizes it all, I can't help but glance over the plastic edge of the cocoon I know belongs to Jack. I stand on my tippy-toes to get a better look, but find only an empty seat and a crumpled blanket left on top of the vacant chair.

He must have already disembarked. We missed him.

The attendant catches my eye, a knowing smile crossing his face. "The guest in that seat has already left the plane," he says. "But he travels with us often. I hope you will, too."

I nod, surprised that I'm disappointed to have missed another conversation with the mystery man. Maybe I'm so broken up over Travis that I'm grabbing onto the first man who crosses my path. The thought of Travis makes my eyes water. He's probably training Stacey on how to handle small marmosets right now, even though the woman has no certifications whatsoever.

Why did I leave my life behind? Maybe I've made a huge mistake.

"Madam?" the attendant says. "If you'll follow me, we'll connect you with your driver."

I'm frozen in place, and my legs won't move. If I step off this plane, I'm really doing this. There's no going back.

Come on, Rebecca, I think. *Hold it together.*

Beside me, Joe barks. He grabs the edge of my sweater and pulls me forward like he knows whatever is ahead of me is better than what we're leaving behind.

"If you say so, bud," I tell him. My legs start moving again, and I follow Joe down the aisle of the plane. The attendant guides us over a ramp and into another VIP waiting area, where a woman in a brightly colored dress waves at me. Her long blonde hair is tied back in braids, and she looks to be in her early thirties. She's holding a sign that says "Welcome

Rebecca Orange!" She waves at me like she's genuinely excited to see me. Something about her demeanor makes all the fear exit my body, and for a moment, I feel completely at home.

"Rebecca!" She squeals, pulling me into a hug. "How was the flight? Was everything okay?"

"It was," I say, nodding. "And just to clarify— you're— Maggie?"

She hits her forehead like she's forgotten a huge detail. "I'm so daft. Yes, I'm Maggie, I should've introduced myself."

"No, I recognized your voice from over the phone! I just didn't know the driver would be you," I tell her honestly. "I was expecting some guy in sunglasses and an SUV with tinted windows."

Maggie laughs. "Typically we *would* send Enrique with the van, but—" she pauses, thinking. "Can I be honest?"

"Always," I tell her.

"I could tell on the phone you were nervous about this, and I get it. It's a huge change. A new country. I thought if I met you myself you might feel better. You know, because you have a friend here."

Suddenly, I want to hug her again. Instead, I look up at the ceiling. "That means a lot," I say. "It really does."

She gasps as she notices Joe, crouching down to his level. "And this must be Joe!" She scratches his head, getting the spot behind his ears that he loves the most. Joe's foot beats the ground as he leans into her hand.

"This is my guy," I say, proud of how perfect he is. "You wanna see a trick? Joe! Earthquake alert! Drop and cover!"

Joe jumps into the air, then crouches down with his paws over his head, butt in the air as if he's covering himself from potential falling debris.

"Good boy!" Maggie says, her laughter echoing throughout the room. "You guys get Earthquakes all the time in California, don't you? You won't have to worry about that here."

She grabs my suitcase and wheels it behind her, and suddenly we're exiting the airport. Bright sunlight floods my eyes as Maggie guides us to a black SUV parked in front of the airport.

"So you *do* have a black SUV?" I tease her.

"I mean, we *are* working for the royal family," she says, suddenly serious. "There are definitely some perks."

She throws my luggage in the back, and before I know it, Maggie, Joe, and I are speeding down a coastal road, windows down, moonroof open. As we drive, Maggie gives me a tour of the country.

"The beaches are beautiful," she says, motioning out the passenger side window. A white, sandy beach expands into the distance, and the water of the Mediterranean is the clearest blue I've ever seen. Seagulls flap overhead, their wings crisp and clean like sails against a cobalt sky. "The castle is a bit more inland, but it's only an hour drive to the sea. That's the thing about Monrovia. We're a small country—smaller than the state you just left behind. So you can get to everything pretty easily."

She makes a turn, exiting the coastal highway and proceeding down a road that moves inland. Rolling green hills expand into the distance, cows and sheep grazing peacefully behind low fences. "So much of our exports are agricultural," Maggie says. She motions out the drivers' side window, where an orchard of trees expands toward the horizon. "We're known for our olives. They're the best in the world. There's something in our soil that makes them taste better. You can't duplicate it."

We make another turn, and suddenly we've entered a small village. "Welcome to the Village of Atwood," Maggie smiles at me.

It's a quaint, European town. The streets are narrow,

marked by cobblestone roads. Pastel paint covers the buildings in shades of sky blue, salmon pink, and sage green. There's a cafe on every block, and groups of people dine al fresco style, enjoying coffee and pastries in the sunshine. The village seems to have invested in extensive landscaping, and there's no shortage of trees, shrubs, and even vining plants that weave their flowers over walls. Wrought iron fixtures dominate everything, from the lamp-posts to door handles.

Joe sticks his head out the open window, his massive tongue rolling around in the fresh air. A few pedestrians point at him, marveling at what a unique dog he is. This happens to Joe quite frequently as he's such a rare breed.

He turns to me, a twinkle in his eye. He loves the attention.

"The village of Atwood is about a thousand years old," Maggie says making another turn. "Obviously we've made upgrades in that time, but we've kept much of the original charm."

She rounds a corner and suddenly we're crossing a stone bridge, trees obscuring my view of what's ahead. As the trees fall behind, the object before us becomes clearer:

It's an enormous castle, connected to the village by the bridge we're crossing. It's built from ashen stone, its peaks and towers painted a crisp shade of blue. Arches mark its entrances, and a defensive wall in the back protects the castle from attacks.

"Welcome," Maggie says proudly, "... to Monrovia Castle."

CHAPTER
Five

WHEN WE ARRIVE at the castle, Maggie wastes no time making sure I'm comfortable. She leaves the SUV parked outside, motioning to a group of attendants wearing all white. "Rebecca's bags are in the back! Get her all set up, would you?"

The attendants descend upon the SUV like ants. Maggie loops her arm over mine and leads me up the front steps of the castle toward a pair of enormous wooden doors. Joe is on my heel, drooling in the warm summer sun.

"Monrovia Castle is one of a dozen royal strongholds in Monrovia," Maggie says, pushing the doors open, revealing an enormous foyer. I'm surprised by how warm the interior of the castle looks. I was expecting all stone walls and cold, ancient art. Instead, it's been decorated in gold trim and patterned, chipper fabrics, a chandelier dangling from the ceiling. The decor reminds me of the French rococo style, flamboyant and extravagant in its attention to detail.

"The biggest castle in Monrovia belongs to the King and Queen, and it's called *Castle Glorieux*. The King and Queen live there, and we have a hundred similar castles spread throughout Monrovia for their relatives. Other members of the Royal Family are in charge of the smaller estates like this one," Maggie says, pulling me down a hallway.

"This is a *smaller* estate?" I gasp, sure that the castle's square footage must rival that of a small city.

"I know," Maggie agrees. "This is a special castle because it was actually the first one ever built. It's the oldest, and that's why it gets the name *Castle Monrovia*, after our country, but we call it Castle Atwood because— in our minds— this place really belongs to the village and the people here. We're hoping to give it its own renaissance. To be honest, the previous Duke of Atwood never cared much for Castle Atwood and let it fall into disrepair, given running an estate is such a huge undertaking. He preferred to spend time on his yacht, sailing the Mediterranean. He was hardly ever here and barely put any funds into maintaining the place. It's only recently we've started to round a corner, thanks to the fact that once the Duke died the King and Queen created a new title and gave it to their nephew, who now holds the title of Duke of Atwood. He's had his work cut out for him getting the place back in working order. He has a whole new idea about what being Royal means, and he's taking this place in a different direction. Something more modern and for the people."

"What's he like?" I ask as we stroll down the hallway, passing paintings on the wall that feature men and women in fancy dresses and military garb. "The Duke, I mean."

"He's fantastic," Maggie says, her voice a little too enthralled by mention of the new Duke "I was so worried when the old Duke passed away and the King and Queen named their nephew as the new head of the estate. I mean, he has quite a reputation—"

"What kind of reputation?"

"That he's a party boy. Always off spending the royal money. Constantly sighted with some young Hollywood starlet. I thought he'd sink us, but instead, he's changed everything around here for the better." She points at a beautiful marble archway that marks the entrance to a stunning sitting room. French doors let in the light, opening up to a sprawling rose garden. "He had the whole place fixed up. New electrical has been put in. An interior designer came to furnish the castle, modeling it after the original style of the time but with a modern twist. He even renewed the rose garden and fixed all the plumbing." She looks around to make sure no one is listening, then leans in, whispering, "I heard a rumor the money allocated for repairs by the Queen and King wasn't enough, so the Duke took out of his own funds to clean the place up."

"Wow," I nod, surprised. "That's commitment."

"It is," Maggie agrees, stopping at a pair of French doors in front of us. "We've done so much construction and improvement. And the last step is the animals, which is why we're so glad you're here."

She throws open the doors, revealing acres of land. A green expanse of grass sprawls into the distance. Tall trees border the private lawn, which ends only when it hits the edge of a mountain. A barely visible brown fence marks the end of the castle's land. In the middle of the space is an enormous barn. Outside the barn roam different species of antelope, zebra, and—

"You have a *giraffe?!*" I laugh out loud.

"Thought you might like him," Maggie smiles. "That's Alfredo. He's a total glutton. Get near him with your lunch and soon you won't have a lunch to speak of. His favorite is pasta. That's why we named him—"

"Alfredo," I say, nodding. The lumbering giraffe stops at a tree, and plucks a leaf from one of the upper branches, turning it over in his mouth.

I walk toward the border fence, resting my elbows on the distressed wood. Joe lets out a bark and leaps over the fence, running toward the middle of the field and rolling over on his back. He positions himself between some roaming sheep, who look annoyed at his presence.

"Is he okay with all the animals?" Maggie asks, concerned.

"Joe was raised alongside cheetahs and lions," I tell her. "He was part of a program to help exotic beasts feel comfortable with humans. He bridges the gap between them and us. He grew up around cats of prey, so if he can handle a cheetah, he can handle a sheep." Joe kicks his feet up in the air, letting out another bark as the sun warms his stomach. "See how he's totally disinterested in them?" I point at my weird dog. "Disinterest is a compliment in the animal world. That's what we want between different species. Which you have a *lot* of." I take stock of the different animals roaming the field. "I mean, zebra have different needs from African antelope. And then you throw a giraffe into the equation..."

"That's why we need your help," Maggie says. "The Duke wants to know these animals are being cared for in the best way possible." She opens the gate and motions for me to follow her. "In the barn, we have the equestrian center, and the birds..."

I can't help but audibly groan. "Tell me you're not keeping the birds with the horses?"

Maggie slides open the door to the barn, revealing a dozen stables for horses. In each stable, an incredible Clydesdale horse whinnies. They're enormous, each one weighing over a thousand pounds. There's a chestnut horse. A sable colored pony. I peak into a nearby bag and find a pile of dried apples. I grab one, crunching it in my hand as I reach out to feed the nearest horse— a midnight black mare. She takes the dried apple out of my head, sighing gently.

"These are purebred Clydesdales," I say, in awe of the graceful beasts.

"Over here we have the birds," Maggie nods. "You can go. They scare me."

"You're afraid of birds?"

"They're like dinosaurs but with feathers," Maggie shrugs.

Leaving Maggie behind, I make my way to the back of the barn, where birds have taken over a section of the barn that's divided off with wire to form a makeshift aviary. There's a beautiful hawk. A sleeping owl. And a handful of smaller species.

"They're all rescues," Maggie calls out. "They were found injured or wounded. Our vets have helped them heal, but none of them can be released to the wild."

I lean down, examining a beautiful red-tailed hawk. The name-tag on his enclosure tells me his name is Ace. He locks eyes with me and lets out a deep caw in greeting.

A knowing lights up my eyes. I have a plan to make this place a haven for animals. Starting with these birds.

"We need an atrium," I tell her. "Separate from the horses and completely independent of the barn. Some place they can have open air and avoid other animals. That's our first order of business. To build an atrium big enough these birds can *feel* like they're in the wild, without actually being exposed to the danger there."

"I'll put you in touch with Phillipe, our head builder," Maggie answers back. "Poor Phillipe's been worked to the bone, but I know he'll be happy to take on another project. And Douglas the groundskeeper might have some suggestions as to location."

Just then, there's a rustling sound from the entrance to the barn.

"What's this I hear about an atrium?" A man's voice says. The voice sounds familiar. I wheel around, discovering Jack, the stranger from the plane who disembarked before I'd been able to say goodbye. He's holding a tennis ball in one hand and throwing it up in the air as he leans against the edge of the barn. Beside him stands Joe, a pleased look on his face. It's as if he's saying, *Look, Mom, I found the man you thought was attractive.*

"It's— you?" I sputter before collecting myself. "I thought we lost you back on the plane. I'd hate to think you're following us."

Maggie clears her throat. "Um, Rebecca, I'd meant to introduce you two at dinner. This is the Duke of Atwood."

"*You're* the new Duke?" I say, my mouth dropping open. Jack seems to blush, his cheeks turning the faintest shade of red. "Just call me Jack, that's fine—" he says.

"I don't get to call you Jack!" Maggie protests, laughing a little.

"That's because if the King and Queen come by and they hear you call me Jack, they'll disown me at once and shut the whole place down," Jack throws her the tennis ball. I get the impression they're supposed to be running a formal operation, but instead, there's a brother and sister type of camaraderie here. They like to tease each other. "That's something you should know," he says, turning back to me. "The King and Queen— my aunt and uncle— they're always looking for a reason to shut us down. When the previous Earl of Atwood passed, they were ready to retire Monrovia Castle. Just knock it down and stop pouring money in. But I managed to convince them to let me take over. I begged them to give us another chance, and now, here we are, a year later."

"Thriving!" Maggie says.

"Surviving," Jack corrects her. "But every month we get closer to making the case that we deserve to exist. And helping these animals—" he motions out the barn doors at the sheep grazing in the grass. "Is an important part of the plans I have for Castle Atwood." He steps toward me and takes one of my hands in both of his, applying a light, friendly pressure. "Which is why I'm very grateful you're here."

He smiles at me, then releases my hand. "Whatever Rebecca needs, Maggie, I'll see that it's approved." With that, he disappears through the sliding barn doors, and the place feels a little emptier for it.

"He's always doing that," Maggie sighs. "Leaves me a task and then disappears."

"Where does he go?" I ask. Beside me, Joe leans on my leg, letting out a little whine as if he already misses his new best friend, the Duke of Atwood.

"His study or the library mostly," Maggie shrugs. "The man spends most of his time with his nose in a book." She loops my arm through hers again. "Should we show you your new quarters then get some lunch?"

"My *quarters?*" I repeat, nervous to see what I'm in for. "It looked fine in the photos…" I think back to the zip file of images I'd been emailed upon signing on. They'd shown pictures of a sad, tiny room with a single bed and a lamp in the corner.

"Oh no!" Maggie laughs, hitting her forehead as if she's forgotten something. "I haven't updated the welcome packet. Those photos I sent you were of the *old* staff quarters. Wait until you see the new ones… Don't worry." Maggie pats my hand. "You're going to love it."

I try to believe her, but based on the pictures I saw, I seriously doubt I'm in for anything good.

CHAPTER
Six

"THIS *CAN'T* all be for me," I say, staring at the sprawling space in front of me. My "quarters" are more like a luxury apartment in any major American city. There's a large kitchen with marble countertops. A spacious living room with sliding doors out to a garden that features the peaceful sound of running water thanks to a tiered fountain. Milkweed grows just outside the doors, attracting butterflies. The living room space is already furnished with massive shelves for books, positioned across from a flat screen TV mounted to the wall and a working fireplace ready for when winter arrives.

"Wait until you see the bedroom," Maggie winks at me, leading me into the next room. Joe follows us, and when Maggie opens the bedroom door, he runs toward the four-poster, king-sized bed and leaps on top of it, rolling over on his stomach. Overhead, a white canopy creates a dreamy effect. A huge floor-to-ceiling window looks out over the grounds. There's a vanity with built-in lighting pressed against the wall, and beside it, a door leads into the master bath.

"Great closet, right?" Maggie says, opening the door to a

walk-in closet. It has multiple hanging areas and plenty of folding space. My clothes are already hanging neatly within, my empty suitcases pushed against the wall. The attendants must have unpacked them.

"The tub is my favorite part," Maggie says, flicking on the bathroom light. A claw-foot soaker tub beckons me, surrounded by white tiles with golden flecks of glass baked within.

"Am I *dreaming*?" I say, looking out the massive windows. From this angle, I have a view of the castle across the shared lawn. It looms in the distance, welcoming in its grandeur, only five hundred feet away.

"When we did the remodel the Duke insisted we completely rebuild what used to be called the servants' quarters," Maggie says, standing beside me and motioning to the castle in the distance. "The quarters were originally built separate from the castle to create delineations between people of different so-called 'classes.' We thought the remodel should even the score a bit."

"How many square feet is this?" I exclaim, still in shock. I was prepared for nothing but a modest bedroom. Now, I'm in Real Estate heaven.

"The entire building dedicated to the staff is about thirty-thousand square feet. But your quarters? About eight hundred square feet," Maggie says. "Not huge, but I'm hoping it will do."

"An apartment that size in San Diego costs four grand a month!" I tell her.

Maggie laughs, then holds up a set of keys. She drops them in my hand. "This key is for the entire building, including the front door. This one is for your individual room. And *this* one—" she points to an electronic fob. "Is for the amenities."

"Amenities?" I ask, heart racing with excitement.

"There's a full gym in the back of the building, plus a jacuzzi and swimming pool on the roof." She pats my arm, still smiling at my shocked expression.

"My apartment is just down the hall if you need anything! Apartment number 9."

"Got it," I say.

"Get some rest you guys," she says as she moves to exit. "Maybe tomorrow we'll go into town and I'll show you the best of Atwood Village. It's the staff's day off, so everyone will be headed to the village. Afterward, we can come back and get started on the bird aviary if you don't mind working a little on a Saturday."

"It's not work if you love it," I tell her.

"We'll get Phillipe, our head builder, to sketch out a quick plan and estimate the cost," Maggie says. "I'll schedule it so Pashmina can attend as well. She's head of castle finances and hates spending money on anything, so get ready to be persuasive."

"Please," I tell her. "Persuasive? Look at Joe's face. Who can say no to that?"

Right on cue, Joe lets his tongue drop out of his mouth, tilting his head to the side.

"Perfect," she says. "See you guys tomorrow!"

I wait until I'm sure she's closed the door behind her, and then I let out a little scream, running into the living room and jumping on the couch. Joe follows me, tail-wagging, and together we celebrate the best decision we've ever made in our lives.

I throw open the French doors that lead into the shared courtyard, enjoying my own little piece of the garden. Butterflies flap around the milkweed, and the sound of the delicate fountain makes me feel right at home.

I take a seat on a bench in the yard, and Joe leaps up beside me, taking up more room than I do with his enormous haunches. He licks my face as if he's thanking me for being brave enough to take a risk on a new adventure.

"Tomorrow we're going to see the best of Atwood Village," I tell him, scratching his ears. "But honestly, bud? I don't see how it can get any better than this."

"OH MY GOD, IT GOT BETTER," I murmur out loud, my mouth full. It's the next morning, and after a *glorious* night's sleep, I'm standing in the dining area of the staff building, eating a serving of fresh fruit with ice-cream on top. But not just any ice-cream. *Rose* flavored ice-cream. Freshly made by the castle chef, who's standing at the back of the room, arms crossed.

Maggie sits next to me, devouring her selections from an enormous continental breakfast spread. She's chosen a croissant with melted cheese on top, folded ham within.

"Delicious, isn't it?" she says, still chewing. She nods across the room at the woman with the crossed arms. She's in her early seventies, with beautiful salt and pepper hair that's been tied up underneath a plump white hat. "Chef Renauld gets up early each morning and makes breakfast for all of us. She's a complete professional. Been doing this for decades. She could run a kitchen in any five star restaurant but she stays at the castle because, well—"

"Because this place is *amazing,*" I say. "She even remembered Joe!"

At my feet, Joe licks up the last of his breakfast, which consisted of left-over steak chopped into tiny pieces, served over a bed of white rice. He licks his lips in satisfaction then looks up at me to scope out any leftovers I might be able to offer.

No dice, bud, I think, shaking my head. I ate my entire breakfast and didn't leave a thing behind.

A woman walks by, typing urgently into her cell-phone. Maggie waves at her. "Pashmina!" She calls out. "Come meet Rebecca. She's our new animal trainer."

"Nice to meet you," Pashmina says, nodding at me in a bare approximation of a greeting. She's in her late fifties, and appears to be on top of her game. There's an essence of corporate power about her that takes me aback.

"I've set up a meeting for us today to talk about funding for a bird atrium," Maggie says to Pashmina who rolls her eyes.

"Perfect," Pashmina says. "I'm *so* looking forward to it." She marches off with an urgent gate, and I can tell from her tone of voice she's very much *not* looking forward to it.

"Never mind her," Maggie whispers. "Pashmina worked for the Earl before the new Duke came onboard, and she's just used to an old way of doing things. She's in charge of the castle financials and the renovations are expensive which has created quite a bit of work for her, but she'll get over it eventually."

Just then, Chef Renauld walks over and places a hand on my shoulder. "Is everything to your satisfaction?" she asks.

"This ice-cream is incredible," I tell her honestly.

"I infused the rose flavor from flowers grown in our very own rose garden," she says proudly before walking away to check on other members of the staff.

Maggie points across the breakfast spread at a man wearing a bright, green construction vest. "Phillipe!" She calls, waving him over. "I want you to meet Rebecca. She's our new animal behavior specialist."

Phillipe comes over holding his plate in one hand. He reaches out for a handshake, which I gladly return. There's a warmth in his eyes— he's the kind of person you like immediately.

"So nice to meet you," he says. "I hear you want to create an atrium for the birds?"

I nod, imagining what we could build together. "That's the first project," I agree. "You're going to make all of their lives better."

"That's the idea," Phillipe says. "We keep improving the property and building, even if some people are up in arms about it."

The comment strikes me as out of left field. How could anyone hate the improvements they've made here?

"Some people don't want you to improve the castle?"

Maggie shrugs, shaking the idea off. "It's the Royal Family. People are always going to have something to say about whatever we do."

"So what brought you to Monrovia?" Phillipe asks me, leaning against the table. "Maggie tells me you're a very accomplished animal trainer. Must have been quite a journey to leave all that behind and join us here."

Suddenly, a lump forms in my throat. I think about Travis, and the fact that our relationship is over. It's not the fact that it's ended that bothers me— maybe it's more that it never really *was*. What he's done seems to invalidate the entirety of our time together, as if we were never real to begin with. Images flash through my mind of the Safari Park and the job I loved. All of it's over now, like it never existed.

"I guess I'm just looking for a new start," I say, and I'm horrified to feel my eyes watering, a choking sound rounding out my vowels. *Don't cry, damnit.* How embarrassing. Phillipe notices my emotion, and he pats my hand, a deep understanding in his crinkled brow.

"I've had more new starts that I can count," he says, his voice deep and syrupy. "Ones I thought I'd never recover from. I've gotten quite good at telling when someone's about to come out of a tough place better than where they started... and you?" He smiles at me. "You're on the right track."

"Thank you," I say, really meaning it.

"We'll meet up later today," Phillipe grins, standing up and clapping his hands together like he could get started any minute. "Let's make a plan for your project. It's going to be wonderful," he assures me, a twinkle in his eye. "I can promise you that."

There's something about Phillipe that makes me believe he'll keep his promises. Maggie nods at me sympathetically. She knows my backstory, but has also learned enough about me so far to know not to bring it up. "We need a fun trip," she says. "Girls day out!" She throws her hands in the air like she's at a dance party.

When breakfast is finished, we hop in a car and head for Atwood Village, just Maggie, Joe, and me. The man in the driver's seat is named Enrique. He wears a small cap that's tilted to the side, and a very somber expression. Maggie leans over from the backseat and pats his shoulder. "Enrique's been working at the castle for the past thirty years, isn't that right?"

Enrique offers a gruff snort in response. "Thirty years but it feels like a different place nowadays."

Maggie laughs, turning to me. "Enrique's not happy with changes the new Duke has made around here."

"How could you not be happy?!" I exclaim, mouth dropping open. "This place is like heaven."

Enrique shakes his head. "The Royal Family is expected to show propriety. When I was young, working for the Royals was a privilege. Not a—" He waves a hand in the air at nothing in particular. "Not a vacation at a theme park."

"Come on, Enrique" Maggie sighs, leaning forward. "You have to admit the new staff quarters are incredible."

"They spent too much money on building," Enrique shrugs. "I was fine with the way things were. But what more is to be expected from *le duc casse-cou?*"

"The Daredevil Duke?" I translate, putting my attempts to learn the language to the test.

"He's just spewing garbage from the tabloids," Maggie shakes her head. She glances out the window, taking in the beauty of the Village of Atwood. "We've arrived!" She smiles, clapping her hands together. "Let's go, team. Enrique, we'll be done in a couple hours." She opens the door and Joe hops out, his paws landing on the cobblestone street with ease.

We spend hours touring the quaint village of Atwood. It's the most charming place I've ever seen in my life. Most of the businesses sell locally made goods, and there's a multitude of places to dine and enjoy the beautiful weather. Maggie fills me in on the history of Monrovia, which was a British Colony for some time before they gained independence. Many of the shops sell Olive products, from crushed Olive spreads to authentic olive oil. Apparently olives are their biggest export. An adorable cafe called *Cafe de Flore* features flowers crawling up the outside wall. There's a purse shop, a bakery, and even an animal supply shop. I make a mental note to stop there later for supplies. We make a quick trip into a cute store featuring tea pots, kettles, and cups in the window. I purchase a beautiful teapot with butterflies painted on its surface, excited at the idea of using it in my new apartment.

We pause at a small newsstand, and I purchase a magazine filled with gossip about movie stars and— according to a picture on the front of the King and Queen— the Royal Family itself.

"Ug," Maggie clucks at me. "You're not really going to read that thing, are you?"

"I need to catch up on the latest gossip if I'm really going to become a Monrovian," I tell her.

On our way back to the car, villagers stop us multiple times to ask if they can pet Joe. He obliges, loving the attention.

"Joe's a new local celebrity," Maggie says. "If you're not careful, he might end up in that magazine you bought!"

Later, Enrique picks us up and takes us back to the castle. The car stops outside the gates, where a man in a red coat and a traditional, tall black hat stops us. He appears to have a sword holstered to his belt.

"Good-day, Cadet Monroe," Enrique says as he rolls down the drivers' window.

"Who do you have with you?" Cadet Monroe peers into the backseat, looking skeptically at Joe, Maggie, and me.

"Maggie and our new animal specialist, Rebecca Orange."

A stern expression crosses Cadet Monroe's face as he looks through a list on his clipboard. "I don't have her credentials."

"I'm emailing them as we speak!" Maggie says, clearly annoyed. "But for now, she's my guest—"

"Make sure she gets a badge," Cadet Monroe cuts her off. "We've had some increased activity this week in terms of threats."

"I'll get her a badge," Maggie agrees.

"And you?" He looks at me dubiously, like I'm a terrorist or a spy. "Make sure you abide by the rules of this property. Understood?"

"Yep," I say, not sure I understand at all but deciding it's better to pacify him.

Cadet Monroe offers a somber nod then opens the gates, and our car heads back toward the castle.

"He's the head of security and he takes his job too seriously," Maggie sighs. "Pay him no mind. I'll get you a badge right away so he can't give you a hard time." She types urgently into her phone, addressing the issue before she forgets.

"Thank you," I tell her. But the Cadet's words still strike me as odd. *An increase in threats from who?* I think. But I shake the question off, because this place is perfect, I can't wait to get started on our new atrium. Nothing bad could ever happen here.

CHAPTER
Eight

"SOMETHING BAD HAS HAPPENED," Pashmina says, her hands shaking. She's dressed in a grey suit set, a cell phone in one hand and a stack of files in another.

"What do you mean?" Maggie says as we walk through the hallway toward the castle grounds. "Was the Duke not able to approve the construction—"

"It's not that," Pashmina answers, her eyes welling with tears. "Not money. I've already called the Police. I couldn't help him. I tried but it was too late to help him—"

Maggie speeds up, trying to keep pace with Pashmina, who's frantically leading us toward whatever has her panicked. She throws open the doors to the garden area.

"Chef Renauld found him. She was heading to the garden to harvest herbs for tonight's dinner when—"

Pashmina goes silent and then, I see him:

Phillipe, the head builder, lying underneath a tomato plant, his face concealed by the vines. His chest doesn't move up and down. Instead, he lies motionless in the dirt.

Joe whines and hides behind me, trying to obscure his enormous body behind my legs. I can feel that he's shaking, and his fur bristles on the back of my knees. *Leave it to the world's largest dog to be afraid,* I think, reaching out to pet him with my own trembling hand.

Maggie gasps, crouching down next to Phillipe. She puts her hand on his wrist, seeking a pulse. She finds none.

"He's dead," she says, hardly believing the words herself. Pashmina lets out a sob, covering her mouth with a hand.

I take a step back, my mind reeling. I can't believe the warm, gentle man I met this morning is lying dead in front of me. He was so kind when he assured me this new start would be good for me. *This can't be happening,* I think, my breath quickening.

Pashmina dabs at her eyes. "We were supposed to meet to discuss your atrium. He was probably out here taking measurements." Tears run down her cheeks. "If I hadn't told him to get started without me, maybe I could have helped him. I was on a call about the castle's tax bill and it went longer than I expected..."

"There's nothing you could have done," Maggie says, choking back tears of her own. "You called the Police?"

"They're on their way. Cadet Monroe is prepared to meet them. He's leaving his post at the gate."

"How could this have happened?" I say, putting my hand on the top of Joe's fuzzy head to stabilize myself. I'm suddenly feeling weak in the knees. "We just saw Phillipe this morning. He was at the breakfast table. He was going to help me build a new space for the birds..."

"Rebecca, you need to sit down," Maggie says, leading me to a nearby iron bench. I let myself collapse onto it, panic flooding through my body.

"We just saw him this morning and he was *fine,*" I say. "Did he have any medical issues that you know of?"

"No," Maggie said. "I updated his file just a few months ago and there was nothing wrong."

"Do you think it was an accident?" I ask, hoping that no one would intentionally hurt Phillipe.

"It wasn't an accident," Maggie says suddenly, her eyes wide. She points at a vine of the tomato plant, and for the first time, I noticed that it's been wrapped tightly around his neck.

"Someone strangled him," she pauses, her body in shock. "Rebecca, I think— I think he was *murdered.*"

CHAPTER
Nine

HOURS LATER, and we're all gathered in the Castle's enormous sitting room, which Maggie has informed me was crafted as a receiving room for dignitaries. Now, it's the holding area for the staffers, who are all waiting to be interviewed by the Police. Everyone mills about, whispers and murmurs filling the space. Joe sits close to my side. He can feel the tension and wants to stay near me. He leans his fuzzy shoulders against my legs.

Maggie speaks into her cell phone, pacing around the room while doing urgent damage control. "I *understand* that but yes— we had to call." She pauses, listening to the voice on the other end. "There's no denying the incident now that it's on the Police scanners. They'll know something happened at the castle. I think our best move is to get ahead of it." The voice on the other end says something that comes out like one long, vapid bleat. "No, I haven't spoke to the Duke yet. He's—"

The door to the sitting room opens and Jack appears, looking horrified and exhausted.

"He's here," Maggie says into her cell phone. "I'll have to call you back." She slips the phone into her pocket as Jack approaches us. He sits on the couch across from me, practically melting into a pile of a person.

"Phillipe— I can't believe it," he says, his face flushed. "Who would want to hurt him? And in our own garden."

"I've just gotten off the phone with the Royal Family's publicist," Maggie sighs, shaking her head. "Apparently they're very concerned about the impact this could have on the perception of the monarchy."

"Of course they are," Jack rolls his eyes, pushing his glasses higher up on his face. "It's just like them to be more concerned about appearances than the death of a man." He shakes his head, still reeling. "Phillipe was by my side from the day I arrived at Castle Atwood. He was there for me when no one else was. He believed in what I'm trying to do here." The Duke lets his head fall into his hands helplessly, then looks back up at us. "I've let him down."

"You couldn't have known this would happen," I say. "No one could have known."

Joe jumps off the seat next to me and moves to the couch the Duke is sitting on, taking the opportunity to lean against him and invite a warm scratch. Jack accepts, running his hand through Joe's long, golden fur.

"Still, I'm in charge of this place," the Duke says, unwilling to let go. "Everything that happens here is my responsibility." He looks at the ground, collecting himself. "Maggie, has anyone reached out to his family?"

"I've sent Enrique to visit them," she says. "His sister lives in the village and will want the news. I thought it was best if one of us went in person rather than over the phone."

"Thank you," the Duke answers gratefully. "I'd also like to meet with his sister here, at Castle Atwood, and have her as my guest as soon as possible. Can you see that it's arranged?"

"Of course," Maggie nods, taking furious notes on her phone.

"And you," the Duke offers me a weak smile. "I fear I owe

you an apology. You've only just arrived, and the place is in chaos. I can assure you, nothing like this has ever happened at the castle."

"I believe you," I say, even though I'm secretly wondering if I've stepped into a pile of mud by coming here. It was off to such a great start, I knew it had to be too good to be true.

"I hope we haven't scared you off, then?" the Duke says, looking a little sheepish.

"Please," I wave a hand at him. "I used to express the anal glands of monkeys once a week. This is nothing."

The Duke gives me a quizzical expression, like he has no idea what I'm talking about and would rather not know. "That's— uh— interesting," he says, clearing his throat.

I can't believe I brought up monkey butts, I think to myself, wishing I could disappear from the embarrassment.

Mercifully, the doors to the sitting room open, and a Police Officer enters, followed by Cadet Monroe, who's still wearing his ridiculous traditional hat.

The room quiets immediately, and all eyes turn to the Police Officer, who's wearing a badge that indicates he's the chief of the department. The middle-aged man clears his throat.

"Thank you all for your patience," he says. "We've invited you here to explain the procedure we'll take moving forward. After speaking over the phone with representatives of the King and Queen of Monrovia, it's been made clear that— per the Royal Declaration of Discretionary Districts made in 1897 — Castle Atwood is considered Royal Property immune from the typical laws governing surrounding law. In short, the Royal Family reserves the right to conduct their own investigation."

Murmurs echo throughout the room. The staff clearly has mixed feelings about this new revelation.

"In keeping with that right, the Royal Family has chosen to

assign the head of the Atwood Village Royal Guard, Cadet Monroe, as lead investigator in this instance."

Cadet Monroe puffs up his chest like he's just been elected the President of the world. Now, the murmurs around the room grow to outrage. There's shouting from the rest of the staff. At the back of the room, Chef Renauld uncrosses her arms and lets out a single, horrified gasp. Next to her, Pashmina— the head of the castle finances, immediately protests. "It would be better for the Royal Budget to rely on public services..." She starts to say, but her voice is drowned out by multiple protests around the room.

Cadet Monroe steps forward, his tall stature allowing him to loom above the group.

"I've been empowered by the Royal Family to immediately terminate anyone who doesn't cooperate with this investigation."

The muffled protests stop, allowing, once again, for silence.

Cadet Monroe loops his hands behind his back, pacing in front of the crowd with a meaningful, skeptical glare.

"Phillipe was killed in the garden, and I know for a fact these grounds are secure, considering I ensure their borders myself. Which means someone here... is a murderer. And it is my intention to discern *who*."

The Duke stands, marching toward Cadet Monroe. "Cadet," he says, as Cadet Monroe takes a formal stance. Even with his new found power, the Cadet doesn't dare disrespect a member of the Royal family. "Is this really necessary?" Jack turns his back to the crowd, trying to create a private moment between him and Cadet Monroe. "No one on this staff is a murderer. I trust all of these people with my life. There has to be another explanation."

"I'm afraid there isn't," Cadet Monroe says. "And, respectfully, your Highness, I now answer to the King and Queen.

They have given me my orders and I am obliged to carry them out."

Jack steps back as if Cadet Monroe has insulted him. There's a pause as Jack takes in the Cadet. "We'll see about that," he says. With that, Jack marches out of the room with a sense of purpose in his step, leaving all of us to face Cadet Monroe.

The Police Officer shakes Monroe's hand. "You have our resources available to you as you please. We encourage inter-departmental cooperation. I'll get back to you with the results of the autopsy report."

The Officer exits and Cadet Monroe surveys the room, clearing his throat as he reaches into his pocket, pulling out a notebook.

"Thankfully for all of us, Phillipe's murder occurred on a Saturday, and much of the staff was still visiting Atwood Village at the suspected time of the murder. I keep immaculate records of entrances and exits to the property via our badge system—"

Maggie leans over and whispers in my ear, "Of *course* he does." She rolls her eyes, clearly annoyed at Cadet Monroe's self- importance.

"That leaves only a few of you behind as possible suspects," Cadet Monroe continues. "If I state your name, please stay behind. The rest of you are dismissed." He opens up his small, black notebook.

"Chef Renauld," he announces. At the back of the room, Chef Renauld leans up against the wall. The only reaction she offers is a brief eyebrow raise as if to say, *what's it you?*

"Maggie Lefevere," Cadet Monroe says, making eye contact with Maggie.

"Here," Maggie confirms.

"Rebecca Orange," Monroe says, scanning Joe and me the same way he did when we drove through the gates earlier in the day. Even though I knew my name was coming, the announcement feels like a punch to the gut.

Great, I think to myself. *I've graduated from single, unemployed midlifer to murder suspect in a foreign country. Things are really looking up.*

"Enrique," the Cadet announces, searching the room for the driver but not finding him there.

"I sent him to the village. He's informing Phillipe's sister," Maggie says. "He should be back any minute now."

"Hmmmph," Cadet Monroe snorts, as if Enrique's absence is somehow evidence of his guilt. He looks back at his notebook, scanning the names, there.

"Monique Charmont?" he says. There's a small sniffle from the corner. A woman dressed in a maid's uniform holds a tissue up to her nose. It's clear she's been crying.

"Douglas Edwards," Monroe continues, his eyes landing on a man in a pair of denim overalls. There's dirt on the knees of the pants, implying he was working outside recently. He offers nothing to Monroe but a nod of recognition.

"Tracey Fields?" Monroe reads the next name on his list. A hand raises on a nearby couch. A young woman in workout gear nervously makes eye contact with Monroe. Her arm muscles are so defined, I suddenly feel the need to do a few pushups.

"And finally, Pashmina Sayers," Monroe concludes, nodding at Pashmina, who looks as if she smells something terrible. Her expression says she hates the idea of wasting money on something as stupid as an investigation led by Cadet Monroe, but there's little she can say or do to stop what's already in motion.

"If I didn't call your name, you're free to leave," Cadet Monroe says. "The rest of you, stay put."

There's a scraping sound as chairs are pulled out and the occupants of the room make a mad rush for the door. They bottleneck at the exit but eventually manage to make their escape, leaving the few of us who were called out by name alone in the room, which feels empty in their absence.

"Now," Cadet Monroe claps his hands. "I'd like to speak to each of you individually. First up, our newest member of the staff..."

I brace for it, already sensing what's to come. "Rebecca Orange?"

I nod at him, my mouth dry.

"Come with me."

CHAPTER
Ten

SWEAT ROLLS down the inside of my right arm, landing at the crook of my elbow. I'm in a small room that serves as one of the castle's many studies. It's dark, except for a strategically-positioned light on the desk that Cadet Monroe has pointed straight at me. The curtains have been drawn, and the effect is something straight out of a noir movie. Beside me, Joe whimpers, putting his head in my lap. I scratch his ears thoughtfully. I don't have anything to be afraid of because I haven't done anything *wrong*. Still, I'm nervous.

"Rebecca Orange," Cadet Monroe says, hovering over me with his massive frame. He's standing while I'm sitting, and the power balance feels uneven. "What brought you to employment at Castle Atwood?"

"I just needed a change," I offer, shrugging my shoulders. I'm not about to tell this man in a funny hat that my boyfriend left me for our dog-sitter. "Spicing things up a bit I guess. I saw the job posting and it looked exciting."

"Uh-huh," Cadet Monroe said with a tone that indicated he very much doubted my story. "And what is your purpose at the castle?"

"I'm supposed to work with the animals and make sure

the facilities support their needs," I say, scratching Joe's ear in my lap to stay calm. Cadet Monroe is completely unqualified for the task he's been given, and I know if he smells any sign of weakness on me, he'll take it as an indication of guilt.

"Do you find it interesting that you were scheduled to meet with Phillipe only mere minutes after he was killed?" Cadet Monroe asks, scanning my face for any reaction.

"I find it horrifying," I say honestly, holding my head up high. "I hate the idea that if we'd been there a little bit earlier, we might have saved him."

"Are you aware that my security gate records entrances and exits?"

"No," I answer. "How would I be?"

"You entered the gate at 3:45pm exactly, and Phillipe was dead by 4:15pm. That's just enough time to commit the murder."

I shake my head, unable to believe someone so stupid has been put in charge of such an important matter. "No offense, Cadet," I say, hoping to stay on his good side. "But you're a very smart man."

He pulls at the collar of his blazer, indicating he agrees.

I clear my throat, hoping to talk sense into him. "So you've of course realized that— as the newest arrival here at the castle— I didn't even *know* Phillipe. I just met him this very morning. Which means I have no motivation to kill him whatsoever. I'm your *least* likely suspect."

Cadet Monroe leans back against the desk, his eyes widening. It's clear he hadn't thought of any of this and was intending to make me his number one person of suspicion.

Not today, you moron, I think to myself, biting my tongue to keep from saying it out loud.

"I'm sure," I continue, "That because of your extensive experience in detective work, you're looking into potential suspects that could have had a *motive* for killing Phillipe, such as revenge, jilted lovers, financial gain." I pause, letting all of this marinate in his tiny, primordial brain. "That *is* what you're looking for, isn't it?"

"I ask the questions here!" Cadet Monroe says, pacing in front of the desk. I've frustrated him, but at least managed to stop him from treating me like public enemy number one.

I can't help but enjoy that I've frustrated this buffoon of a man. There's nothing more pleasing than watching an arrogant person trip over their own assumptions.

"Why was it that you managed to evade official registration through the office of Security upon your employment?" Cadet Monroe asks me, leaning forward.

"Official regi— what?" I ask, alarmed. "Maggie took care of all the paperwork when I was hired on, but the whole process was rushed. If there were steps to take, she would know them."

Cadet Monroe lifted a file off the desk, opening it to view the contents within. "It appears here you were cleared by the employment office, but— as Maggie can attest— all new employees are required to be registered with the Office of Security for my personal inspection, and in order to receive a badge. And yet, I've received no paperwork for you."

"It must be an oversight," I say, shrugging.

"And you were unaware of the process?" He asks, still doubting me. Cadet Monroe is clearly the dangerous sort of person who locks onto an idea and can't let it go. At the start of our conversation, he was convinced of my guilt. Somehow, I've managed to move him in a new direction, but the suspicion still lingers.

"Of *course* I was unaware," I say, almost laughing out loud. "Cadet Monroe, I've never worked at a castle before, let alone this one! How would I have any idea what your internal processes are?"

"*Internal...*" he says, stroking his beard.

Joe catches my eye from the floor, an alarmed look in his expression as if to say "Is this guy for real?" It's clear to both of us that Cadet Monroe is willing to lock onto any suspicion and see it to its end. For a moment, I'm reminded of a case I heard about years ago on the news. A college student was murdered in a small Italian town, and the Deputy Officer there blamed her roommate for the murder. When asked what evidence he had to make the arrest, the man claimed it was because the girl had dated multiple men in the area, and must therefore be practicing "witchcraft."

The idea is ridiculous, but the girl still spent two years in prison awaiting a trial that ultimately failed. Moral of the story? *It just takes one idiot to ruin somebody's life.*

I glance back at Joe, putting a hand on the back of his neck. It's best we handle this situation with care. Even if Cadet Monroe is a buffoon that would ultimately be proven wrong, he could make our lives miserable for awhile.

"Look," I say, putting my hands in the air. "I know I'm new around here and that makes me seem suspicious, but I really didn't know Phillipe or have any reason to harm him. In fact, him staying alive would have helped me with my job. I needed his assistance to build the atrium." I grit my teeth, hating what I have to do next. But I know I'm in a bad situation, and surviving is my top priority. "And I'm *sorry* if my paperwork was filed incorrectly," I almost choke on the fake apology for something that wasn't even my fault. "But I really have no way of knowing how things are supposed to be done around here. I'll talk to Maggie about it tonight and make sure you have all my paperwork at the Office of Security."

Cadet Monroe stares at the ceiling like he's trying to solve a puzzle. Then, he states slowly, "Maggie was with you in the car when you returned earlier today. Where had you two been earlier?"

"We went to town like everyone else," I shrug. "It's everyone's day off and Maggie wanted me to see the village even though she scheduled our work appointment with Phillipe for later in the day."

"Maggie scheduled the appointment with Phillipe—" he says, mulling the words around in his mouth.

"Of course, because she schedules everything around here."

"And she forgot to send me your paperwork..."

"Maggie's really busy," I say, not liking where this is going and feeling the need to defend my only friend in Monrovia. "She's trying her best but I can see she's doing a job that would ordinarily take ten people. She's the Duke's de facto assistant, she runs the castle, she oversees all of the staff. It's so much—"

Cadet Monroe sits on the edge of the desk, legs crossed. "Interesting... and has Maggie told you she is dissatisfied with that arrangement?"

"Wha—" I stammer, realizing that I've unintentionally led him down an incorrect trail. "No, of course not. Maggie loves her job."

"Does she?" Cadet Monroe asks the question, but it's clear he isn't looking for an answer. He paces again, scratching his chin. "What we have here is a dissatisfied employee who's been overwhelmed handling the recent building projects. She's pushed to the brink, but she can't quit because she needs employment. She's tired, but the work keeps coming. The Duke's renovation scheduled has her pushed her to the edge and she decides, in a fit of rage, to take action!" He pauses, stopping in his tracks. "How convenient that the head builder is dead, no? All building will cease for some time due to Phillipe's murder. And Maggie... Maggie will have less on her plate. Convenient, isn't it?"

"I really don't think she would ever—"

I start to say, but Cadet Monroe raises a hand in the air to silence me. At the sight of the Cadet's raised hand, Joe lets out a low, rumbling growl. He thinks Monroe is threatening to hit me. All at once, Joe leaps to his feet, baring his massive, slobbering teeth straight at the Cadet. This is what Tibetan

Mastiffs were bred for, but I'm still surprised to see Joe jump into action. Usually he only does complicated behaviors for a piece of cheese.

Cadet Monroe takes three steps backward, almost tripping over his feet as he moves away from Joe.

"Joe!" I say, pulling on his collar to get him to sit. "Sit! Settle." Joe offers a sit followed by a lay on the ground, but he never once takes his eyes off Cadet Monroe. "Sorry about that," I say. "He was nervous."

Cadet Monroe slicks his hair back, then strides across the room with his chest puffed out. He opens the door.

"You're free to go," he says, practically pushing Joe and me out into the hallway. He's had enough of us, and it shows. But what he said about Maggie stays with me, a nagging feeling that he's identified a new suspect churning in my stomach.

I can't leave without saying something.

"Listen," I stop at the door frame, turning to face Cadet Monroe. "Please don't waste time investigating Maggie. You're on the wrong trail here. I don't know why someone killed Phillipe, but it was someone with a *motive*. Maggie just doesn't fit the bill."

Cadet Monroe smiles like he's just won the lottery. "Then why are you so eager to defend her?"

With that, he slams the door in my face, leaving Joe and me standing alone in the hallway, utterly shocked at what's just happened. In trying to make things better for Maggie, we've only made them worse.

What have we done?

CHAPTER

Eleven

HOURS LATER, and my worst fears are confirmed. Joe and I are sitting in the living room of our quarters, reading a book, when there's a knocking sound at the door.

Please let it be Maggie, and let her say everything's fine, I think as I open the door.

"Everything's terrible," she says. Just as I suspected, it *is* Maggie on the other side of the door, but she's definitely not fine. Her eyes are red from crying, and she sucks up a bit of snot between sobs. "Monroe thinks I did it. That massive, terrible idiot thinks I did it."

I pull her into a hug and then usher her into the living room. "He really is a massive idiot," I say, feeling a pang of guilt churn in my stomach. "Let me put on some tea and we'll sort this out," I tell her. There's a steaming sound as I place the teapot I purchased in the village onto the stove, eager to offer Maggie any sort of comfort.

Joe jumps on the couch and lays his golden head in Maggie's lap, inviting her to scratch his cheeks. She does, and it seems to make her feel better if the sound of her dwindling hiccups is a reliable indicator. "He thinks I'm guilty. He said I'm overworked and that I must have murdered Phillipe in a fit of rage. As if I'm just some—" she hiccups, "... *emotional* crazy person who murders perfectly-nice-people at the drop of a hat! Do I *look* like an emotional crazy person to you?"

I don't answer right away, because the truth is that she looks like a hot mess. Her hair is tangled in a low bun. Her cheeks are bright red. There's snot on her nose. But she looks better than I would if I had someone like Cadet Monroe out to get me.

"You're not a crazy person," I say, passing her a china cup filled with tea, two lumps of sugar on the side of the plate underneath it. I pair it with a dollop of spiced honey, which I've learned is traditional in Monrovia. "Cadet Monroe is the crazy one."

"He said he's '*not going to let me out of his sight.*'" She leans in and points a finger at me, offering a pretty spot-on impersonation of Cadet Monroe. Even Joe looks alarmed at the sudden change in Maggie's cadence. Her voice lowers to a perfect impression of Cadet Monroe's disarming baritone. "He said he's going to '*prove that I'm guilty and make sure I'm not just fired, but that I go to prison for what I've done.*'" She drops the impression, leaning back on the couch, miserable once more. "I can't believe this is happening," she groans. "And right when everything was coming together."

"What do you mean coming together?" I ask, feeling there's something important to learn underneath what she's shared.

"I'm not supposed to say anything," Maggie hiccups again. "But the Duke has big plans for this place. The renovations haven't been for nothing. We were so close to announcing his plans, and now, it's all ruined."

"What kind of plans?"

"I should really let the Duke tell you," she waves a hand in the air. "I think he's quite impressed with you. He'll want to show you himself." She sighs, taking a sip of her tea. "I can't believe an idiot like Cadet Monroe is going to ruin my life."

"Well, um," I struggle to find the words. "That might actually be our fault," I say, glancing at Joe. Joe makes a whining sound and looks at me if to say... "*us?*"

"Okay, fine," I roll my eyes, setting down my cup of tea and taking Maggie's hands in mine. *It's now or never.* "Maggie, I'm afraid that when I was in there, I said some things that came out wrong. Cadet Monroe made me so nervous because I'm new and he mentioned that my papers hadn't been filed with the Office of Security—"

Maggie shook her head. "Him and that stupid Office of Security! You know that's just something he invented right? I humor him and send all the paperwork and I sent yours—" she pauses, a horrible idea striking her. "Oh my God. I never sent yours." She slaps her forehead. "I've been so busy with the remodeling of the castle exterior wall and the bridge and — I never sent your paperwork for the badge! I wrote the email when we were in the car but I didn't actually send it."

"It's fine," I say, shaking my head. "The point is, Maggie, I accidentally did something awful. When I pointed out that I didn't know anything about the paperwork it turned him onto you, and now he won't let it go. He thinks you were overworked by all the changes around the castle and he made up this crazy story that you might have killed Phillipe."

"What?!" Maggie cries. "That's crazy. I would never kill someone over being tired at work."

"I know," I assure her. "But Cadet Monroe is on this trail and he thinks you might be the murderer. And it's my fault."

"This isn't your fault," Maggie says. "It's Cadet Monroe's fault. And maybe mine as well." She sighs, leaning back on the couch and rubbing her temples with her fingers. "He's hated me from the day I started here, possibly because I never took him or any of his requests seriously. And now look where it's gotten me." Her voice shifts to a whisper, as if she's afraid we're being listened to. "And honestly, the King and Queen are to blame here as well. They trust an old way of doing things, and to them, Cadet Monroe is part of that old guard. Even though he's an idiot." She pauses, taking a moment to rest her face on Joe's forehead. Joe helpfully licks her nose, getting rid of the last hints of snot, there. "It's awful that I'm going to lose my job, but even worse to lose it because of an idiot like Monroe." She glances up at me. "But I'm really glad to have made a friend in you. Don't feel bad about Monroe. It's me who should feel bad, bringing you all the way over here for nothing."

"What do you mean for nothing?" I say, suddenly alarmed.

Maggie sits up straight, surprised I haven't put everything together. "Isn't it obvious? The King and Queen are going to use this as an excuse to pull the plug on the Duke's plans for the castle. Maybe not today, but soon— they'll stop funding us and the whole thing will go under water. They've been waiting for an excuse and the PR fall out from this will be a nightmare. I can see the stories in the press now! 'Duke mismanages estate.' 'Murder at Monrovia Castle: Taxpayers Funding Castle of Death!" She sighs, pulling Joe into a hug again. "We'll all lose our jobs anyway. And me? Hopefully I don't go to prison. I don't wear jumpsuits well."

A slow simmer lights up in my stomach. Flashes of injustices in my own life play through my mind like a film reel. Travis appears, telling me he's leaving me for Stacey. Images of packing up my desk at work, all because one man had decided he'd had enough of me. The thought of Maggie suffering a similar fate makes me outraged.

"Why should *you* lose your job just because Monroe is incompetent and somebody who works here is a murderer?"

"Um..." Maggie chews on her bottom lip. "Those seem like really big reasons that could lead to job loss."

"They're *small* when compared to your talent!" I shout, standing up and repositioning myself in front of the couch like an orator in front of an audience. Joe raises his head out of Maggie's lap, perhaps hoping I'm going to give him a treat.

"We can't let arrogant Cadets or stupid ex-boyfriends be in charge of our destinies. No, we're not going to let idiots who decide to sleep with the dog-sitter determine our fates!"

"I feel like this is about more than Cadet Monroe..." Maggie murmurs.

"It *is* about more than Cadet Monroe!" I exclaim, crouching down next to her. "This is about every woman everywhere who's seen her own life get worse through no fault of her own, just because one jerk thought he was right when he was actually *wrong*."

"I just don't know what to do about it," Maggie says, her eyes watering again.

"I do," I say, standing once again. There's a passion building up inside me I haven't felt for a long time. It's the same passion that made me want to become an animal trainer, and it's based on the belief that my purpose in this world is to make life better for all living beings. "I'm going to solve this murder, and you and Joe are going to help me." Joe wags his tail at the mention of his name, showing he's pleased with the proposition. "Together, we're going to find out who *really* killed Phillipe. And we're going to collect irrefutable evidence so that when the time comes, our conclusion puts Cadet Monroe to shame. We're going to save our jobs, make sure you don't have a criminal record, and protect the castle from being defunded." I hold out my hand, waiting for her to shake it. "Are you with me?"

There's a pause as Maggie considers, and then, she takes my hand in hers. "I'm with you," she agrees.

"Joe?" I ask.

His tongue hangs out for a second, and then he throws a paw in the air, his massive toes landing over our hands. The look in his eyes says he's not quite sure what he's agreeing to, but he's in all the same.

"Let's do this," I say, and together— I believe we can.

CHAPTER
Twelve

"IF WE'RE GOING to do this, I need some pasta," Maggie says, rubbing her stomach. A growl from my own stomach seems to agree, so we head into town for a delightful meal of fresh pasta and a few glasses of red wine from a restaurant in the village. I order the ravioli, Maggie gets the Carbonara, and even Joe has a little plate of his own spaghetti, thanks to the kind proprietor who fell in love with him at first sight. We eat at an outside table off to the side of the cobblestone walkway, talking about the murder case the entire time. Once the incredible meal is finished, we get the dessert to go. Now, we're seated in my living room, two giant cannolis in front of us, whipped cream and all. Joe is sulking in the corner because he didn't get his own cannoli— but Maggie sneaks him a bite of hers every time my back is turned. Neither one of them thinks I notice it, but of course, I do.

"We need to create a list of suspects," I say, standing in front of a bulletin board I purchased at a supply store at the edge of the village.

Maggie nods, opening up a file in front of her. "I've collected pictures of everyone Cadet Monroe mentioned, along with personal details." She smiles, taking another huge bite of her cannoli. "That's the plus of being in charge of everything," she says, mouth full. "I've got access not just to their employee records, but all the gossip I learn from being around the castle."

"Perfect," I say, nodding. "First up, there's you and me."

Maggie coughs, a bit of cannoli stuck in her throat. "You're not seriously thinking either one of us killed Phillipe?!"

"Of course not," I shrug. "But I'm trying to outsmart Monroe and keep you out of jail. If we're going to do that, it's important to walk through every potential trail he might take."

"Okay..." Maggie says dubiously, passing me two photos and two push pins. The first picture is an eight-by-ten of her face, using the image straight off her employee badge. She's beaming and looks like a model with clear skin and wide eyes. Typical Maggie. The second photo is my own picture, taken at the passport office before I hopped on the plane to Monrovia. I look a bit haggard and slightly less glamorous than Maggie, but hey, at least I've got attitude. The look in my eye says I'm not someone to be messed with. Channeling that same energy, I use the pushpins to stick both images to the board.

"Perfect," I say. "Two suspects down. Who else did Monroe mention as being at the castle at the time Phillipe was killed?"

"Chef Renauld," Maggie says with regret. She passes me a picture of the Chef. In the photo, the chef is about twenty years younger. Despite her youth in the picture, she still holds herself with the same composure she has today— which tells me Chef Renauld has always been a woman who's grounded in her own strength. "I don't think she would do it, Rebecca!" Maggie exclaims, a sigh escaping her lips. "She can be a little frosty and she had issues with Phillipe, but she's not a murderer."

"Issues with Phillipe?" I ask as I tack the image to the board.

"Small things," Maggie shrugs. "She got annoyed that his building plans kept stepping on her gardens. She's had to move her plants about ten times at this point to make room for castle improvements and remodels. She asked Phillipe to be more considerate, but he was always a man on a mission."

"Huh," I say, trying not to sound like I'm reading too much into this information. Maggie clearly likes the Chef, but it doesn't escape me that Phillipe was strangled with the vine of a tomato plant. If that doesn't serve as a statement from a disgruntled grower, I don't know what does.

"Alright, that's the chef," I say, eager to move on. "Who's next?"

"Enrique, our driver," Maggie says, pulling out a photo of Enrique. "He was with us when we came back to the castle from the village. I don't think he could have had time to hurt Phillipe."

"But we all split up for awhile, remember?" I say, thinking back to earlier in the day. "He dropped us at the front and went to take the car around back. It would be the perfect alibi..." I consider the fact that Enrique had shared with me earlier that day that he didn't support all the changes happening around the castle related to building. The timing was certainly strange.

I pin Enrique's picture to the board next to Maggie's. "Next up?" I ask.

"Monique Charmont," Maggie says, passing me a photo of the woman I saw crying earlier. She was dressed in a maid's uniform and looked genuinely moved by Phillipe's death. "She's the head of the housekeeping department," Maggie says. Then, she leans in, whispering. "The gossip around the castle is that her and Phillipe were more than friends."

"Lovers?" I say, surprised.

Maggie nods, "Which means there's no way she would have hurt him."

My eyebrows raise, and I can't help but shoot a meaningful look at Joe, who's now snuggled on his bed in the corner. He gives me a similar glance, and I know what we're both thinking: how can Maggie be so naive?

"The number one suspect in any murder is the significant other," I tell Maggie, shaking my head. "A jilted lover has a million motivations for murder. Revenge. Rage... or just, you know..."

The desire to make him see what an enormous idiot he's been, I think to myself, images of Travis flashing through my mind's eye. I'd be lying if I said I hadn't wanted to hurt him when he told me he was leaving me for Stacey. *He was lucky there weren't any tomato vines around.* Maybe that's why Travis broke the news to me in a public place— he was lowering his odds of ending up murdered by yours truly.

"I mean, haven't you ever been dating someone and wanted to ring their neck?" I ask Maggie.

"That's true," she agrees. "And the fact Phillipe was stran- gled with a tomato vine does seem personal."

I pin Monique's image to the board, adding her to our collection of potential suspects. "Who's up next?" I ask Maggie, thinking back to this morning. "Wasn't it the man with the denim overalls?"

"Douglas," she says, passing me the man's photograph. "The groundskeeper."

"Did he have any issues with Phillipe?" I ask.

"Not that I know of," Maggie shrugs. "But I am kind of surprised he was still at the castle today. Usually he takes our day off and spends the whole thing off site. I don't know where he goes, but I've never seen him stay behind on a day off. When Cadet Monroe said his name, it struck me as odd that he was still here."

"We'll have to see if we can get him to talk," I nod, pinning him to the board. "Let's see, after Douglas, it was..."

"Tracey Fields," Maggie says, rifling through the folder for another photo. She passes it to me, and I stare down at a beaming image of a woman in excellent physical shape. She's in workout clothes, just as she was this morning, and her hair is pulled back in a high ponytail. Her arm muscles are so strong you can see lines where the biceps emerge. "Tracey's our fitness expert," she says. "She offers personal training to the duke and the staff on certain days. Her yoga classes are Tuesdays in the gym, and she does boxing on Fridays. She's a black-belt."

"So she's capable of killing a man?" I ask.

Maggie rolls her eyes. "Tracey would never!" She pauses, considering. "At least, I don't *think* she would ever kill someone..."

"It takes strength to strangle a person," I think out-loud. "We'll have to see if she has an alibi or a motive."

Maggie nods. She pulls another photo out of the file. "Last one," she says. "Pashmina Sayers, head of castle finance." She passes the photo to me and I recognize Pashmina, who I met earlier today. In the picture, she's dressed in a grey suit, hair sensibly hanging by her shoulders. She looks annoyed at having to take a picture at all— a feeling I empathize with. "She's very professional," Maggie continues, "... and manages all the castle funds. Hardly a murderer."

"We don't rule anyone out until we've talked to them and established a motive and alibi," I say, pinning her picture to the board. "That leaves one more suspect."

"What?" Maggie says, surprised. She rifles through her folder. "No, that's everyone. We got them all."

I shake my head, walking to the bookshelves, where I slid the gossip magazine I bought earlier onto a top shelf. I pull it out, flipping to a story about the Duke. The headline reads: "THE DUKE OF DISASTER: WILL THE PARTY BACHELOR EVER CHANGE HIS WAYS?" Beside it, a full page image of the Duke on a yacht balances out the story. I rip the image from the magazine and pin it to the board.

"The Duke was here all day, was he not?" I ask.

Maggie gasps. "*Rebecca,*" she says, as if I've committed a crime. "The Duke would *never* kill anyone. He's—"

"I can't eliminate a suspect until we get an alibi. Simple as that." I pause, remembering something. "Actually, there's another person no one's considered."

"Who?" Maggie asks.

"Cadet Monroe himself. We know he was at the castle on everyone's day off because he stopped us at the gate. Can you print his picture as well?"

"First thing tomorrow," Maggie nods. She stands, looking at our board of suspects. "That's a lot of people. Who should we talk to first?"

I squint at the board, considering my next steps. "We have to be quiet about what we're doing," I say, considering the consequences of our actions. "If Monroe gets the impression we're snooping around, he might try to stop us. We need a cover story."

"We could say we're just getting our newest employee used to the castle," Maggie says, smiling at me. "That's a cover story.

"Yes," I smile back at her. "Sometimes being the new girl in town has its advantages."

CHAPTER

Thirteen

THE NEXT MORNING, Maggie meets up with Joe and me outside the staff quarters, all three of us prepared for our first real investigation. We eat a short breakfast under one of the castle's many arbors, enjoying pastries and coffee at a table situated under vining wisteria while talking strategy. The scent of the flowers infuses the morning with a hazy calm. For the first time in a long time, I feel hopeful.

"So I'll introduce you under the guise of being a new staff member," Maggie says, her mouth full of croissant. "We'll try to present it as non-threatening.'

"Exactly," I say, taking a sip of my coffee and slipping Joe a bit of my raspberry pastry under the table. He snaps the bit of food up with his enormous tongue, and it disappears in an instant. "The goal is not to let anyone know what we're up to, otherwise, they could go to Cadet Monroe and ruin it all. Or worse..." I pause, afraid to say the horrible thought out loud.

"What?" Maggie asks. "What's the worst?"

"Well,"I shrug, stating the obvious. "There's a murderer among us. If they find out we're trying to catch them, it paints a bit of a bullseye on our backs, doesn't it?"

There's a funny gurgling noise from under the table, and I

look down to see Joe's head turned to the side, his eyebrows arched as if he's alarmed by what I've just said. I reach down and scratch his ears. "Don't worry bud," I say. "You're safe with me. I've got a plan." The look in his eyes says he'd like to see this so-called plan, preferably put down on paper and with an insurance policy in place.

"Should we get started?" Maggie smiles, jumping up from her seat and brushing crumbs off her crisp, white pants. "Is it weird I'm kind of enjoying this? I've never done anything but be an assistant to Royalty, and now I'm an assistant to a *detective.*" She grabs my hand and pulls me out of my chair.

"I'm just a lowly animal trainer," I say, laughing.

"I wasn't *just* talking about you," Maggie says. "I was talking about Joe over here. He's in charge of the investigation after all."

Joe paws at her with one of his enormous feet, hoping for more croissant.

"Oh yeah, he's a regular Sherlock *Bones*," I say.

"Oof, that was a *ruff* one," Maggie laughs as we make our way across the grass and toward the castle, ready to interview our first suspect.

———

Monique Charmont is a tougher nut to crack than I expected. When I first met her during Cadet Monroe's gathering of the suspects, she looked fragile, a wisp of a thing crying in the back of the room. Now, in an immaculately-pressed housekeeper's uniform, she's a force to be reckoned with. Her dark hair is tied up in a bun, and a badge on her shirt that reads "Head of Housekeeping" announces her authority.

"She wants to *shadow* me?" Monique asks Maggie, aghast. She barely looks at me, acting as if I'm not even here.

"Yes," Maggie nods. "Rebecca is the new castle lead on animal welfare, and she's shadowing every department to gather information on how our activities at the castle affect our animal brethren."

"What could cleaning possibly have to do with animals?"

"Well," I say, leaning in to explain. "Different cleaning products can actually impact the animals more than you'd think. Certain chemicals present a problem, not to mention the sanitation processes can create noise that interrupts natural biorhythms."

Monique grunts, her body language communicating she doesn't particularly care about biorhythms.

"I'll be an extra pair of hands," I tell her, holding my palms up. "You can put me to work. Joe, too." Beside me, Joe offers a helpful pant.

Monique takes us both in, debating, then, she reaches into her cart and pulls out a pair of rubber gloves, which she tosses my way. "Fine, she says. But we're here to work. No monkey business."

Joe looks up at me with his ears pinned back, which is a sign that he's absolutely planning on getting into *monkey business.*

An hour later and Monique and I are scrubbing down one of the castle hallways together, two spray bottles of cleaner in our hands. She plays music from a little portable radio positioned in the corner of the room, an Italian opera blaring. It's difficult work, but at times therapeutic. There's something that feels good about cleaning up a mess when you can't control much else in life. My rag moves in circles over the mahogany walls, rubbing wood polish into the smooth, burgundy surface. Joe naps in the corner, helpfully minding his own business.

"This song makes me think of my ex-boyfriend," I say, nodding at the little portable radio. "My Italian isn't great so I'm not sure what it's saying, but—"

"It's saying love is difficult," Monique answers, her voice stern and brusk, but also wavering underneath. Monique strikes me as a strong person who's holding back deep emotion. "The lyrics speak of a man who loves a woman, but he cannot bring himself to commit to her fully. He enjoys his freedom too much. A tragedy, no?"

"Definitely," I tell her honestly. "Did Maggie tell you why I came to the castle?"

Monique shrugs. "Not Maggie, but Phillipe mentioned there was a new staff member who was *le coeur brise*. One with a broken heart." She stops wiping down a credenza in the hallway long enough to look me up and down. "From the sadness about you and the fact you only recently arrived, I knew it was you."

Gee, thanks, so glad to know I have a sadness about me, I want to say, but I bite my tongue. I'm getting somewhere with Monique. If Phillipe told her about my breakup, that means she saw him on the day he was murdered. He'd only just found out my circumstances that morning, which means they'd spoken in-between breakfast and the moment he was killed.

"Heartbreak is a terrible thing," I sigh, hoping our mutual situation will give us something to bond over.

Monique glances at me, and for a moment I'm worried she might yell at me. But instead, she breaks down, leaning against the wall, sobs rattling her shoulders. "*Oiu,*" she agrees. "Heartbreak is a terrible thing. And one must carry on. One has to carry on."

It's a bold move, but I drop my rag, walking toward Monique and pulling her into a hug. Beside me, Joe arrives at her leg, nudging her with the top of his head. She chuckles weakly, reaching down to scratch the top of his head. "*Je suis desolet,*" she says, wiping her eyes. "It is not the Monrovian way, to show such emotion."

"You're fine," I tell her, shaking my head. "Of course you're upset," I say, ready to test the waters. "I assume you and Phillipe were... you know... more than co-workers."

She nods. "We tried to keep it quiet, but people in the castle talk. He was a beautiful man."

"I have to agree," I tell her, thinking about how Phillipe comforted me the morning he was killed. "I only met him briefly, but he was so empathetic. He understood what I was going through." I pause, hoping now's the right moment to ask her my most important question. "Monique," I lean in, serious. "This may sound crazy, but I keep thinking Phillipe's death had something to do with all the building around the castle. Did he say anything to you?"

Monique looks at the far wall, a searching expression on her face. "So many of us support the changes the Duke is making," she sighs. "Under his new plan, my role would see me supervising only. I'd get promoted. Once Phillipe knew that, I swear he tried to build faster," she laughs, thinking fondly of the man she loved.

"But did he tell you of anyone who had a grudge against him? Anyone he made angry?"

Monique blows her nose into her cleaning rag. "Nobody," she says. "The man was the most lovable person. There was no one who could have such a problem with him."

She stretches her arms toward the ceiling, leaning down to grab the bucket of water by her feet. "We should get back to work," she says, motioning down the hallway. "Three more rooms await."

My biceps already hurt thinking about polishing the walls of the rooms at the end of the hall, but I begrudgingly agree. Joe falls into step beside us, and as we walk down the hall, I desperately search for any way to keep Monique talking.

"I think about my ex-boyfriend often," I tell her, hoping she'll take sympathy on a heartbroken co-worker. "I wish there were some way to bring us back together after a big fight," I lie. I'm hoping she'll reveal whether she ever fought with Phillipe. Her grief seems so genuine I'm almost ready to eliminate her as a suspect, but I'd like to be absolutely sure before striking her from the list. "Did you and Phillipe have a way to make up after a fight?"

A cheeky grin crosses her face as she turns to answer me. "The same as any couple makes up after a fight, no?" She winks at me. "But no, the physical is not enough. Phillipe was a true romantic. He wrote me letters after an argument, and even though he could have handed it to me, he slid the beautiful notes under my door. Not just when we fought you understand, but other times as well. He wouldn't use cell phones, and hated text messages or calls. The man wrote me letters as if he were deployed at war. *Tres romantique.*" She hooks the bucket she's carrying onto one arm, freeing up a hand to pat my shoulder. "Perhaps you should write your ex a letter, no?"

Phillipe wrote her letters, I think, realizing I've stumbled onto a gold mine. If I can get my hands on those letters, it's possible Phillipe could tell me something useful in his own words.

"I'll think about it," I tell her, knowing the next move I'm about to make is a risky one. "I don't suppose there's any way you'd let me read the letters Phillipe sent to you?" I ask her, trying to seem innocent. "For inspiration?"

She takes her hand off my shoulder, her face flushing. "Absolument pas!" Monique exclaims. "They are too private. Between lovers." She makes a clucking sound and then returns to her cleaning. But her denial makes me double-down on my gut instinct.

I have to find a way to read those letters.

CHAPTER
Fourteen

LATER, Maggie and I meet up at a cafe in the Village Atwood, and I fill her in on everything I learned from Monique over two glasses of wine and a charcuterie board. Our little table is positioned on the cobblestone street, two chairs arranged at an angle. On a third chair sits Joe, looking like a human because of the way he's sitting with his feet pulled under his stomach, his chest out proudly, nose pointed toward the table. Pedestrians point as they pass by and the waiter gives me a dirty look.

"Joe, *down*," I insist, but he doesn't budge until I pick up a piece of cheese in offering. Finally, he leaps onto the cobblestone walkway and settles there.

"So Phillipe wrote Monique letters?" Maggie says, resting her chin on her hand. "That's so *romantic*."

"Romantic, yes, but it could also help our investigation," I answer, crunching on a cracker dipped in locally-sourced olive oil. The olive oil in Monrovia is unlike any I've ever tasted— smooth and bright all at once, with absolutely no bitter after taste. I can see why it's the export they're most known for.

"There could be so much in those letters that's relevant," I consider. "They could tell us whether he and Monique had a fight, or if he ever cheated on her. They could also tell us if there was someone in the castle that held a grudge against him. Monique said Phillipe preferred to leave her letters instead of sending text messages or making phone calls."

"Do you think we can eliminate Monique as a suspect then?" Maggie asks, excited.

"Her grief seemed genuine," I say. "She appears to have been deeply affected by his murder. But then again, she could just be a really great actress."

"Oh my gosh! I once saw her lie to get more vacation time," Maggie snaps her fingers as if she's suddenly remembered something very important. "She claimed her aunt broke her back and the Duke gave her six weeks paid leave, but her Facebook showed she was on a beach in the South of France."

"So it's possible she's faking her grief," I nod. "But it *did* seem very real to me. I'm not willing to eliminate her yet, but she's not my top suspect either."

Maggie checks her watch, then chugs the rest of her wine. "That's good because I've got you an appointment with another suspect in an hour."

"Which one?" I ask, a little concerned.

"Don't hate me..." Maggie says, and all at once butterflies start to flap around my stomach.

"Maggie," I say, my voice forceful. "Which. One."

"You said you wanted a new lifestyle in Monrovia, so—"

I groan, pushing the charcuterie board away from me.

"If you'd told me, I wouldn't have eaten so much cheese!" I say.

A short walk back to the castle, and before I know it, I'm in the gym of the staff's quarters, meeting our next suspect. Tracey Fields is about six feet tall, has muscles to be jealous of, and the bubbly personality of a fairy in a kid's story. As the head of wellness at the castle, Tracey has dedicated her life to being fit and helping others follow in her footsteps. Her hair is pulled back tight in a ponytail, and she practically jumps up and down when she hears Maggie's cover story about why I'm there.

"Rebecca's a recent addition to our staff and she wants a new life here in Monrovia, and part of that is fitness!" Maggie says.

By "new life" I meant eating croissants, I think, but I keep my mouth shut because the cover story is a good one.

Tracey shakes my hand, moving it up and down too quickly. "I love working with staff members to help them meet their goals," Tracey says. "The Duke and I agree that total wellness should be part of any employment program. So, Rebecca, what *are* your goals?"

To survive a single training session, I think. But instead of saying the truth out loud, I decide to earn her trust by seeming like I could be a repeat customer. "Oh, you know, I'd like stronger... legs. And arms. The whole thing. Just to be— strong."

"We can definitely work on that," Tracey says. She glances down at Joe, who's seated at my feet like he might have to defend me from the monster before us. "And is this plump guy joining us? I bet we could get those paws moving and shed a few pounds!" Joe glances over his shoulder at me, then takes off, plodding across the room and hiding safely in a corner where he won't be asked to move. He lands in a heap, a giant sigh escaping his furry muzzle.

"That's his dog-log pose," I tell her. "He won't get up for hours. Looks like I'm on my own."

Maggie leaves us to our own devices, and Tracey takes me through a series of exercises that get my blood pumping. Music blares in the background, and the entire workout is an hour- long, terrible blur of push-ups, dance moves, sit ups, barbells, and stretchy bands that make my leg muscles burn. As the sweat drips down my brow, I try to remind myself why I'm doing this.

Save your job. Save Maggie's future. Save the castle, I remind myself. But as Tracey puts me in yet another sixty second "plank pose" none of this seems worth it. *Maybe Maggie would do fine in prison!* I think to myself. She'd have free meals and plenty of down time. And maybe I don't need a job! I could just live in my car instead. Still, there's too much at stake, so I shake off the desire to quit, admonishing myself and returning my focus to the plank pose at hand.

Mercifully, the workout ends, the music stops, and I'm allowed to collapse to the floor in something called "corpse pose," which is the only one I've liked so far. Tracey lays down next to me on a yoga mat, demonstrating what I'm supposed to be doing. She's lying flat on her back, arms open, eyes closed.

"So, um, I'm just supposed to sit here in silence?" I ask her.

"This is your time to be with yourself," she answers, putting a hand on her stomach.

"Oh," I say, nodding like that makes sense to me even though it might be the most annoying thing I've ever heard. "But I'm not really by myself, I'm with you."

"Yes, *silently* with me," Tracey nods, placing special emphasis on the word "silently."

"I don't love silence," I tell her, sitting up. "Actually, maybe we could use our last few minutes to talk about *wellness*," I say, laying a trap.

She sits up, taking the bait. "That's what I'm here for," she agrees. "Overall staff wellness."

"See, that's really interesting to me," I tell her. "Because in my old job in America companies don't think that way. It's very rare to find a place of employment where they care about staff well-being to this extent." I motion around the gym at all the exercise equipment.

Tracey smiles. "That's why I wanted to be part of the program here so badly," she offers. "The Duke is changing things. This isn't just a shift for the castle. Because he's Royal, the Duke's plans are about a change in the culture of our country. And I'm in favor of anything that offers people better health. My goal is to make sure every staff member leaves the castle with better health than when they arrived."

"But Phillipe didn't exactly leave with better health, did he?" I ask. Her eyes open wide at my blunt mention of Phillipe, but she doesn't look suspicious or bothered by my line of questioning.

"Isn't that *so* scary," she says while leaning in, her voice a whisper. "What's really wild is I had just been talking about him a few hours before he died and then— bam— he's murdered."

"You were talking about him?" I try to make my voice sound casual. "To who?"

"The Chef," she shrugs. "We work together to plan nutritious menus and she was saying how frustrating it's been trying to cultivate her plants with all the construction. Those plants are her babies, and Phillipe kept bulldozing her gardens without even talking to her first."

"Was she really upset?" I ask.

Tracey shrugs. "Chef Renauld can be hard to read, but I know she was bothered by the fact we wouldn't have tomatoes for the pasta that night, and it's all because the construction killed yet another crop."

"She was specifically upset... about tomatoes?" I ask. "Yeah," Tracey says. "Is that important?"

"Phillipe was strangled with a tomato vine," I tell her.

Tracey covers her mouth, gasping. It's clear she hasn't heard the specific details of how the murder was committed until now. "I knew he was murdered but I hadn't heard *how*!" She exclaims. "Strangling somebody? That's *not* good wellness karma."

"Uhh, no, it's not," I confirm. "I saw him because I happened to be at the castle for a meeting." My voice rises as I try to disguise my interest in what I'm about to ask next. "Why did you happen to be at the castle that day?"

"The Duke wanted a private training session," she says, flipping her ponytail again. "He likes to do TRX every Saturday," she points at cables that have been screwed into the ceiling, a harness nearby for a person to dangle from. "We could try it some time if you want! It's *so good* for your posture."

"I'll think about it," I say brightly, knowing full-well I will never agree to such a torture device. "What time does the Duke train with you on Saturdays? Just asking so I don't step on his appointment," I say, trying to cover my tracks.

"Oh, around three o'clock," she says thoughtfully.

Exactly two hours before the murder, I think to myself. The TRX training doesn't provide an alibi for either the Duke *or* Tracey, given that they both would have had time to kill Phillipe after the session. But my first impression of Tracey is that she has no motive, and is too concerned with wellness to stoop to murdering someone. Still, I can't eliminate her as a suspect. Not yet.

"After his appointment is over you must be pretty tired," I say. "Do you lie down and take a break?"

Tracey laughs. "Me? Never! After my standing three o'clock with the Duke, I stay here and record virtual training videos the staff can access even if they're not able to come to a regular class with me. I'm trying to build an entire online library. See?"

She reaches into the stretchy pocket of her workout pants and pulls out her cell phone, opening up the video album app and passing it to me. On the screen, a video of Tracey on a stationary bike plays. She reminds me of a Peloton instructor as she throws her hands in the air. I check the time stamp on the video— it says it was recorded at four-forty-five p.m. on Saturday.

There it is. A rock-solid alibi. There's no way Tracey could have been recording this video and killing Phillipe at the same time.

"Ooh this gives me an idea!" Tracey gasps. "Do you want to do a quick spin on the bikes?" She nods at some stationary bikes in the corner. "Ten minutes at the end of a workout can really lock in the metabolism boost!"

Using a cue I taught Joe many years ago, I casually put my hand behind my back, moving my finger in a circle, which is Joe's sign for *"bark and return to me."*

There's a deep bark that emanates from the corner, and Joe helpfully stands up, rushing to my side. He paws at my leg as if to say he can't stand to watch anymore.

"Oh gosh, that's so tempting!" I tell Stacey. "But that's Joe's way of telling me he needs a little potty break. Better get him out of here before he has an accident—" Joe gives me side-eye to let me know he hates being used as an out.

I offer Tracey an assortment of "thank yous" and platitudes, finally escaping to the blissful common area of the staff quarters, eventually leading Joe back to our own beautiful apartment. We open up the French doors to let in the clean air, collapsing on the couch together in a ball. I look up at our list of suspects, wondering who killed Phillipe.

Monique's letters enter my mind again, and I can't help but feel there's some secret in them waiting to be revealed. Then, an idea hits me. I think about how Joe's training helped me escape the training session. Why can't I use my skillset in another way?

I know how to get the letters.

CHAPTER
Fifteen

LATER THAT NIGHT, I can't sleep. The duvet cover that's thrown over my legs feels too hot, but the night air without it is too cold. Even Joe— who's usually out like a light— tosses and turns in bed. My arms ache from the workout earlier in the day as I push myself up to pull Joe into a snuggle. Even though he's bigger than me, he's always the little spoon.

"We have too much on our minds, don't we bud?" His fur smells like clean shampoo. I get a whiff of it as I throw one arm over his shoulder. He licks my hand to let me know that he agrees.

The truth is, we've come to love it here. In the little time we've spent at Castle Atwood, it's begun to feel like a place we could belong. The idea of losing our new home before the adventure has even begun is heartbreaking. Tomorrow, I intend to put my plan to get Monique's letters into place, but I'm not one- hundred-percent sure it will work. And even if it *does* work, there's no guarantee the letters will reveal anything useful. Suddenly, in the middle of the night, it feels as if I'm on a wild goose chase, following nothing in particular. The horrible idea that perhaps I'm no better than Cadet Monroe makes me sit up straight in bed, stomach churning. Without delay, I shake the feeling off.

"If we can't sleep, we might as well make use of the time," I tell Joe. My feet hit the floor as I step out of bed, clothed only in my Nirvana t-shirt and pajama shorts. I throw on sneakers and a sweatshirt, grabbing my cell phone to check the time. It's two in the morning. Maggie told me I'm allowed to use the castle library anytime I desire— and because she didn't specify, I choose to believe that includes during the middle of the night.

I open up the French doors that lead to the sprawling castle grounds, and Joe walks tight on my heel as we make our way across the lawn toward the castle. It's a looming figure this late at night, but not in a frightening way. There's something beautiful about its turrets, which spiral toward the sky. We reach the back entrance and the door creaks as I pull it open, stepping into the corridor. Modern sconces on the wall light our path, plush rugs directing us toward the library.

We open the double doors to find a completely empty library. Vast shelves of books line every wall, sliding ladders allowing for access to the highest shelves. Solid wooden tables decorate the space, with seating areas of plush arm chairs collected in tiny alcoves. In the middle of it all, a fireplace crackles, golden flames shooting sparks up the chimney.

I'm surprised to find the fire going this late at night, and double- check our surroundings to make sure no one else is in the library. It's definitely empty, and I consider that maybe all the fireplaces in the castle are on a timer, or tended to in shifts even so late in the evening.

Together, Joe and I creep forward, heading for a particular set of shelves. When discussing the ongoing building, Maggie told me there's a section of the library that contains before and after diagrams of the renovations.

We scan the shelves, and then: we find it. A series of

binders, each one at least five inches thick with a label on the spine indicating which part of the castle renovations it documents. The East Wing. The West Wing. The Foyer. The Courtyard. I stop at a binder labeled "The Staff Quarters" and remove it from the shelf, its bulk heavy in my hands.

I drop the binder on one of the carved wooden tables, opening up to the first page. Joe settles in by my feet, patiently waiting as I skim the binder's contents. The first page indicates that Phillipe was responsible for overseeing the building itself, and for the documentation within. He's taken meticulous notes. As I scan the pages showing the renovations, his handwritten adjustments are everywhere.

I stop on a page that shows the new layout of the staff building, complete with apartment numbers. There's a diagram that shows every unit and its location, size, and design down to every detail, including built-in cabinets and castle-provided furniture.

Suddenly, there's a creaking noise. *The door to the library is opening,* I think. Someone else is here.

Joe rises from my feet, rushing across the room to greet our visitor, who's not yet visible beneath the dim light. I don't waste time thinking. My hands move of their own accord, ripping the diagram of the staff quarters from the binder and shoving it into my pocket. It's just in time, too. A figure steps into the light, his asymmetrical smile familiar.

Jack. The Duke of Atwood.

He's in flannel pajama bottoms and a white t-shirt, his glasses balanced on his nose. There's nothing particularly royal about him at this moment. He leans down, scratching Joe's ears in the place where his fur is all downy fluff.

"Didn't expect to see you tonight, stranger," he says to Joe, glancing up at me.

"I- I'm sorry—" I stammer. "Maggie said we could use the library anytime. I didn't think anyone else would be here."

"It's a welcome surprise," he assures me, stepping further

forward into the light. "The fireplace was me. I was here earlier and just left to get a cup of tea." He holds up a china mug as if to prove his story is true. He approaches the table I'm sitting at, and I have to admit— he looks rather dashing as light from the fireplace casts a golden glow over his face. "I thought I was the only one who visited the library on sleepless nights. The two of you being here makes me feel rather less alone in my compulsions." He sits and Joe immediately leans on him, resting his head on the Duke's knee.

"We tried to sleep but there was too much on our minds," I say honestly.

The Duke nods as if he understands exactly what I mean. "Yes," he sighs. "Nothing like this has ever happened at the castle. I have to say, I feel individually responsible for Phillipe's death. It's my job, you see, as the patron of this land — to make sure everyone who relies on it is safe and secure."

I don't say anything, because I'm struck by the thought that the Duke *could* be responsible for Phillipe's death. He's still on my suspect board, and he was here at the castle at the time of the murder. *We could be alone with a killer right now,* I think, glancing down at Joe, who still has his head in the Duke's lap, tongue out. Still, I like to believe Joe wouldn't take so fondly to a murderer.

"Are you interested in the construction?" The Duke asks. He's noticed the particular binder open in front of me.

"Oh," I say, trying to think of a quick cover story. "Yes, I just— Maggie was telling me there's been big changes happening and I guess I just wanted to know more."

"You should have asked me!" Jack exclaims. "I'd be pleased to share. Give me just one moment—" He stands, crossing the room to a set of bookshelves and removing three large binders within. He brings them back to our table and spreads them out in front of me, pointing to the cover of the first one. "This is my plan for the castle. It will represent my life's work, when it's completed—" he says.

"The Social and Physical Renovation of Castle Atwood," I read aloud. "It's more than just construction?" I ask.

"Much more," Jack agrees. He opens the binder, flipping through a detailed plan that includes photographic representations of his vision. "I want to turn Atwood into more than just a stodgy remnant of times gone by. My vision is that the castle can serve as a model for the new values of modern Monrovia." He flips to a page labelled "PUBLIC BENEFIT," showing illustrated images of happy people milling about the courtyard. "I want the castle to be open to the people," he says. "It should exist for the benefit of the surrounding village of Atwood. I'd like the castle to become a type of community center where we host education events, blood drives, fairs, benefits, and more, all for the public's interest."

"That's— wonderful," I say, completely touched that he would want to share his space with the surrounding village. The idea of a Royal typically conjures images of gated walls and security, not community fairs.

"And even more, I want the castle to serve as an example of an ethical business model." He flips to a page titled *Staff Access and Welfare*. "That's why you see so many new staff wellness programs. I want people who work at Atwood to feel that they're part of an enterprise that gives back to them as much as they give to it. The relationship between staff and company should be symbiotic."

"Well, you've done a great job with that," I laugh. "Between the food and the housing and the free fitness training, the staff here is pretty well taken care of."

Jack pauses, his cheeks flushing. "It's—" He stammers. "You have no idea what it means to me to hear you say that."

I take in the man in front of me, trying to reconcile him with the party-bachelors described in the tabloids. "This might be inappropriate to ask—" I start.

The Duke waves a hand. "There's nothing you can't ask me. Don't you see?" He looks around the library. "I want everything the Royal Family does to be accessible and transparent. That's why the plans I have for the castle are sitting on a library shelf where they're accessible to all, and not locked away in a cupboard for only a few to see."

"It's just..." I say. "I picked up a tabloid in town the other day, and the way they presented you was... They didn't talk about any of this."

"The despicable bachelor story?" The Duke laughs. He leans forward, resting his chin on his palm. His eyes turn glassy, like he's remembering something from a long time ago. "When I was a younger man, I must admit, the story wasn't far off from the truth. But what you have to understand is that I was lost. I was raised in a model that values distance from other people. Being Royal means being separate from your fellow humans. And for much of my youth, I felt quite— lonely. So, yes, I eschewed my responsibilities and lived for any comfort I could find in a given moment, which certainly means I earned that reputation. But I did it all because I didn't believe I could change the system. Then, on my travels across the world and through the books I read, I learned that I was in a position of privilege. That weaker men than me had used their status to change the world. And when I was gifted Castle Atwood, I saw a chance to have a new start. A chance to do something that *matters*. It's as if I've found my purpose."

His passion for the idea seems to create an electric ripple in the air, and I find my heart beating just a little harder.

"That's how I feel about animals," I tell him. "The day I started as a trainer, it was like I saw decades unfold before me. I knew I wanted to help every animal live the best life possible in the conditions they found themselves in."

"Then we understand each other," he says, a charming glint in his eye. He looks at me just a little too long before clearing his throat. "You know, you're very important here. These animals at Atwood are all rescues. Giving them the best life possible is part of our mission. If we can complete it," he adds darkly, his face falling.

"You're worried you won't get the chance." I offer the sentence as a statement, not a question.

"The King and Queen were already skeptical of my vision," he confirms. "News of the murder has already leaked to the press. I expect we'll see the tabloids push the story as early as tomorrow. Then, the fall out will come. Cries about what we're doing with tax payer money. Shouts for the monarchy to be abolished entirely." He sighs, running his hands through his hair. "There's nothing the King and Queen hate more than negative press. The Royal Family exists best when boats are not rocked."

"Would it help if we were able to explain why the murder happened?" I say, hopeful my investigating isn't for nothing.

"Maybe," he sighs. "But with Cadet Monroe on the case, I doubt the odds are in our favor. That man couldn't find— what is the American saying about barns and sides?"

"The backside of a barn," I laugh. "Yes, I'm sorry to say I agree."

The Duke smiles at me like he wants to say more, but then stops himself. He glances at his watch. "Well, I'm afraid I should at least *try* to get some sleep." He pauses, then reaches out to take my hand. "It's been lovely to be in your company," he says before letting go. Then, he bends down to Joe, who's staring up at him with adoring eyes. "And *you* young sir..." he says, reaching toward Joe.

Over the Duke's shoulder, I give Joe the hand signal for "shake." Joe immediately puts his paw in the air and the Duke laughs, offering him a handshake in return. "What a well-mannered young gentleman you have," he says.

With that, the Duke leaves, shutting the door softly behind him. A shiver runs down my spine. After speaking with the Duke, our investigation seems more important than ever.

We have to get those letters.

Moments later, Joe and I leave the library, making the long walk across the castle courtyard back to the staff quarters, thinking all the while about what we've learned. I know I won't be able to sleep tonight, not just because of my new knowledge of the Duke's plans, but because of his passion. Even if the Duke is Royal and off-limits in terms of any romantic prospect, he's made me realize there are men out there that live the way I do— dedicated to a cause they love.

When Joe and I settle into bed, I feel hopeful again. The duvet cover curls around my shoulders, warm and inviting. My new life here has so much promise if I can get the chance to live it. Maybe losing Travis wasn't so bad after all. In fact, by breaking up with me, Travis may have done me a favor.

Just then, my phone buzzes. I reach over to the bedside table, picking it up to look at the screen.

There's a text message from Travis. It reads, simply:

TRAVIS

I made a huge mistake. Can we talk?

My stomach churns. Bile seems to rise in my throat. Without thinking, I open a drawer in the bedside table and shove the phone inside.

"Well, bud," I say to Joe. "Looks like we're not sleeping after all." Joe offers a little whine and pushes his enormous nose close to mine, sniffing my face like he might find answers there.

The mattress seems to sigh as I roll over, trying to push Travis' text out of my mind. Right now, what matters is solving the murder. Tomorrow, I'm going to get those letters.

CHAPTER

Sixteen

THE NEXT MORNING, Maggie meets me in the animal courtyard to help me execute my plan. We work through the standard rotation of animal-related chores together, and in-between brushing the alpacas, I've filled her in on my conversation with Tracey and the fact that we can eliminate her as a suspect. I've also told her about the text message from Travis, but for some reason, decided to leave out my conversation with the Duke last night. I don't know why I feel the impulse to keep the exchange private, except that the moment felt like a dream. Maybe it's because we met so late at night, but something about the interaction between the Duke and I feels fragile. It's as if the entire experience is a wisp of a thing that could be destroyed if examined too closely.

Maggie climbs up a step higher on her ladder, holding up a bowl of Carbonara pasta. She stretches as tall as she can, and there's a slurping sound as the castle giraffe— Alfredo— bends down to slurp up the pasta. The ossicones on the top of his head— what some people call "horns"— graze the top of the bowl as he cranes his beautiful spotted neck a little lower. Maggie gives him a well-meaning pat on his nose.

"You know that's going to stop as soon as I get a proper

animal nutrition plan in place," I say, shaking my head. Alfredo gives me side eye, looking out at me over the edge of the enormous bowl Maggie's holding.

"Chef Renauld makes it fresh for him and it's only three times a week!" Maggie clucks. "I don't see the big deal."

"The big deal is that giraffes aren't supposed to eat pasta," I sigh.

"You heard the expert," Maggie tells Alfredo, removing the almost-empty bowl from his line of sight. The giraffe glares at me as Maggie steps off the ladder, pouring the remains of the meal into the trash. She leaves the bowl beside it and together, we head toward the barn.

"Travis is such a joke," Maggie says as we walk across the grass. Joe lopes in step beside us, his massive paws leaving deep tracks in the dirt. "How dare he text you after what he did."

"He's also tried to call me twice since then," I say, holding a hand up to my face to shield my eyes from the sun.

"Did you answer?" Maggie gasps.

"I let him go straight to voicemail," I say. "I've got bigger fish to fry."

"Fish?" Maggie says, concerned. "I thought we were going to see the birds."

"It's an American expression," I laugh, stopping in front of the barn. Together, Maggie and I pull back the sliding barn doors, stopping to feed the horses dried apples before moving into the back atrium area.

Maggie shivers. "I really dislike them," she says, looking at the birds in the atrium enclosure. "Are you sure there's not another way to get the letters?"

"There probably is, but this is the way that makes the most sense to me," I shrug, pulling a leather glove out of my bag. I purchased the glove in town earlier this morning, along with some dead mice from a pet food store. "Think about it. If a bird takes a letter, who can they charge with theft? Using the bird gives us plausible deniability, plus it keeps Cadet Monroe off our trail."

I put the glove on and make a cooing noise, approaching Ace, the beautiful hawk I first met upon my arrival. He tilts his head to the side, a clever look in his eyes saying he remembers me. Gently, I open the door. He doesn't flinch. With great care, I tie the end of a tiny wire around his leg. I'd expected him to protest, but instead he holds completely still.

"Has he been trained in falconry?" I ask.

"No idea," Maggie says. "They found Ace injured out in the woods. It's possible someone kept him as a pet, even though that's illegal in Monrovia."

"Hmmph," I grunt, hating the idea of not knowing Ace's past.

There's a crunching sound as I hold out my gloved hand, and Ace jumps onto it like he's done this a thousand times. As I pull him out of the enclosure, Maggie backs up, shaking a little.

"He can't get to me, can he?" she asks.

"Be careful," I say. "I've heard a hawk's favorite food is Maggie."

"Haha, very funny," Maggie rolls her eyes.

"I think he's been trained before," I tell her. "He hopped on my hand no problem. This may be easier than we think."

We head for the courtyard, and in no time at all, Ace is in flight. He stretches his wings wide, circling the sun like it's everything he was born to do. I test his recall by making a whistling noise and holding a dead mouse in the air. Sure enough, he glides back down to my arm, swallowing the mouse in a single breath. He's a professional right off the bat, and doesn't even seem to mind Joe's presence. It helps that Joe lays on the ground with a calm, grounded presence. It's Maggie who's nervous. She sits next to Joe, using him as a shield between herself and the bird. Thankfully, Joe doesn't seem to mind. He allows her to sit behind him, panting in the heat of the sun.

"This bird knows what he's doing," I say. "He understands basic falconry. All we need to do is connect that to the letters. Grab the papers?" I say. Maggie retrieves as set of envelopes and blank, folded papers from my bag that I prepared in advance. Staying as far away from Ace as possible, she sets the pile a few hundred feet in front of us on the grass.

"Hit us with the mouse!" I shout to her. Begrudgingly, Maggie reaches into my bag and removes a dead mouse, placing it inside one of the empty envelopes. Then, she steps aside, and I release Ace into flight.

His majestic wings curve across the open landscape, rotating as he cuts low over the letters, picking up the dead mouse and returning to me with it chomped in his beak.

We practice this way for a few hours, gradually advancing the behavior. First, Ace learns to associate the mouse with the letters. Then, he begins picking up the envelopes and papers as a result of their proximity to the treat— there's no way for him to grab one without the other. With a little help from Maggie, we advance to tying the dead mice to the envelopes so they're inseparable. As Ace returns to me with both items, he learns that I'll separate them from each other, enabling him to eat the object of his true desire and allowing me to keep the letters. Finally— after much time has passed and the sun is low in the sky— we advance to the challenge behavior, and Ace learns to pick up the papers without any mouse nearby at all. When he brings the papers back to me, he gets a treat.

"That was amazing," Maggie says, running up to me. "How did you do that?"

"It's all about escalation," I tell her. "You start with behaviors that are natural for the animal, like hunting or preening. Then, you connect those to what you want them to do. You reward them every time they do it right to reinforce the choice and before you know it, they're trained."

Ace's wing's flap as I raise my arm into the air, signaling him to rest on a nearby branch. He obliges, and I leave him safely perched in the tree as Maggie and I go over our strategy. We remove the plans of the staff quarters from my bag, the edge of the page still ripped from my adventures in the castle library. Together, we smooth the paper flat over the grass, examining the layout of the rooms.

"Her apartment number is 218," Maggie offers. "You're sure?"

"I checked it against the employee records."

My finger scans the page, landing on apartment 218. Its window faces the opposite courtyard, and the design layout within shows that the window connects to the bedroom.

"Think she'd leave the letters someplace obvious?" Maggie asks.

"We better hope so," I shrug. "Ace doesn't have opposable thumbs, so opening a drawer would be difficult. But her grief seemed so genuine to me... I have a feeling the letters are out in the open." It's a hunch, not a guarantee, but everything in me believes Monique has the letters in a place where they're easily available. Any person in her position would be re-reading them, missing the man she loved. It strikes me that this might have been too intensive a plan for a simple suspicion, but still, I've gotten us in this deep. I need to see my plan to its end.

"Whether I'm right or wrong, we're about to find out," I say to Maggie. My knees creak as I stand, whistling into the air for Ace to return. His wings flap and he leaves his safe spot on the branch, landing comfortably on the leather glove I've put back on. Near my feet, Joe cocks his head to the side. He looks annoyed that another animal is answering to the sound of my whistle. "It's okay, bud," I tell him. "You're my number one." He gives me a side-eyed glance that says that had better be the case.

The three of us move to the courtyard on the other side of

the castle, and I'm grateful it's dinner time. All the other staff will be downstairs, gathered around the table to enjoy one of Chef Renauld's latest concoctions. The timing means Monique likely isn't in her room either. This is our best chance.

When we reach the area of the courtyard beneath the window for room 218, Maggie quickly pulls a small, black camera the size of a dime out of my bag. She passes it to me I attach it gently to Ace's back using a soft lanyard. We use these cameras at the animal park to observe animals, and they're so lightweight they're virtually unnoticeable.

"Turn on my phone," I tell her, and Maggie grabs my cell phone, opening an app I've showed her earlier. She flips to the video screen, and a live-streamed image from Ace's back shows our enormous faces staring back at us, from his point of view.

"Let's see what he sees," I tell her. I raise my arm in the air, making the motion to release Ace, and he flies upward toward the open window of room 218. On the first pass, he misses it, landing on the edge of an adjacent window. It occurs to me Ace has no idea where I'm sending him, so I grab some twine from my bag and tie a mouse to the end of it. I lasso it above my head then release it, sending it careening through the open window and into Monique's apartment. A quick flick of my arm sends Ace back toward the window, and this time: he's in.

Maggie and I huddle around the cell phone video, watching Ace's progress from his point of view. He balances on the edge of the window sill, then drop-steps into the room, his little feet digging into the carpeted floor. Judging by the way the live-feed moves left to right, he seems to take a moment and look around the room. There's an unmade bed. A pile of clothes in the corner. A half-eaten croissant on the bed-side table, dried out and unappealing.

"Wow," Maggie says. "The place is a mess. I guess

Monique cleans all day and doesn't want to do it when she gets home."

Just then, Ace angles himself toward a dresser that's been pushed against the wall. Its surface is decorated by a wilting fern, and photos in frames of Monique in various locations around the world. There's one of her in front of the Eiffel Tower. One of her by the Pyramids of Egypt. And a charming picture of her and Phillipe, standing in front of the Big Ben Clocktower. Beside the photo frame, something catches my eye.

"Look!" I gasp, pointing at a pile of papers on the desk. "Is that what I think it is?"

"Either that, or we're about to steal a credit card offer," Maggie says, gripping my arm.

Ace seems to have noticed the letters as well. His wings flap, and the video becomes an enormous jumble of images as he glides to the top of the dresser. He clips one of the letters in beak, then soars back out the window, returning to my arm with a victorious landing.

We grab the letter out of his mouth and check the signature. Sure enough, it's from Phillipe.

"I can't believe that worked," Maggie says, jaw-dropping open. "How did you *know* it would work?"

"I didn't," I shrug. "Just following a hunch."

I offer Ace a dead mouse for his contribution to our case, then quickly photograph the letter with Maggie's cell phone. Without delay, we send Ace back up through the window, repeating the process multiple times until every letter has been captured and photographed. When we've got them all, we decide we need to return them to the room so Monique isn't suspicious. I tie the letters in a bundle, passing them to Ace and raising my arm to send him off in flight. He soars through the window, and the video on our bird-camera shows us that he drops them on the floor near the dresser before turning back around to make his way back to us.

"Close enough," Maggie says.

"She'll think they fell off the dresser," I agree. "Hopefully, she explains it away." I give ace a final mouse to thank him for his service. "This was a long day, buddy. Let's get you back to the atrium for some sleep."

We return to the barn and Ace gives me a quick nuzzle with his forehead before returning to his enclosure, where he hops up on a perch and immediately closes his eyes to enjoy a nap. The interaction was positive for Ace. Birds of Prey need constant stimulation, which is why training sessions are so beneficial. And I'm hoping the letters prove to be useful for us as well.

Thank you, Ace, I think before making my way back out of the barn, where Maggie and Joe are waiting for me.

"We better get to dinner before anyone gets suspicious," Maggie says. "It's not like me to miss a meal. They'll *know* something's wrong if I'm not scarfing down Chef's beef and potato soup."

"We'll go through the letters together tomorrow morning," I agree. "I'll print out the pictures and we can read them at the same time— see if we find anything."

We grab our bags and leave the barn exactly as we find it so no one is the wiser. Even if someone *did* see our training session, I've created a cover story that involves training Ace and stimulating his mind through behaviors.

Maggie, Joe, and I make our way back toward the staff quarters, trying our best to look as if we haven't been up to anything. The scent of dinner wafts through the doors, and suddenly, my mouth is watering. I swear every day at the castle gets better and better in terms of the meals, but even if tonight's dinner is fabulous, I'm sure there's no way Chef could beat last night's risotto.

"OH MY GOD, it's even better than the Risotto!" I practically shout, shoveling another spoonful of beef stew into my mouth. A savory, almost gravy-inspired stew base melts in my mouth, tender beef and soft potatoes brushing against a crisp, tomato flavor. "Chef, you have no right to make food this good. This should be illegal."

We're seated in the spacious staff dining room at a long table. Almost the entire staff has decided to eat at the castle tonight— apparently the Chef's stew is a group favorite. The room is crowded and the comforting sounds of conversation and laughter fill the space, but Chef still managed to hear my praise.

Across the table from me, Chef smiles. She tries to hide it, but Chef Renauld takes pleasure in her own talent. She's an excellent cook who knows it, and from the pleased look on her face, she never gets tired of seeing other people react to her meals. "It was nothing," she waves a hand in the air in mock deference. "An easy recipe to throw together."

"I highly doubt it," I shake my head. "Easy is opening a can. This is *art*."

"Tres bien," the Chef says. "The key is the ingredients, you know. Things taste different when they are freshly picked." She leans in like she's about to tell me a secret. "The produce is grown here at the castle. That's what sets it apart. The tomatoes were just harvested, picked only at the prime of their cycle. I check them every day."

The tomatoes, I think, my stomach suddenly turning as I remember that Phillipe was strangled by a tomato vine. My eyes scan the long dining room table that spans the length of the eating hall. Everyone here is a member of the staff, and it occurs to me that almost every subject of our investigation is present. Enrique, the driver, sits at the end of the table, with Monique by his side, the two of them chatting animatedly. Tracey, the fitness expert who I've eliminated as a suspect, sits on the other side, talking to a staff member I haven't met yet while flexing her bicep as if to demonstrate a workout move. The groundskeeper— Douglas— eats alone, not speaking to anyone. Almost in slow motion, he shovels one spoonful of soup into his mouth after the other. Douglas is on my list to interview, but I haven't had the opportunity to get him alone yet.

I'll try to corner him after dinner, I think to myself, making a mental note to keep eyes on him.

Finally, on my side of the table, Chef Renauld is seated directly across from me, and Pashmina and Cadet Monroe are positioned just next to Maggie, who's to my right. Pashmina is on her phone, which doesn't surprise me. The woman constantly seems to be working, always messaging someone or on a call. Her phone is practically another appendage, like an arm or a leg. I don't think I've ever seen her without it.

"Put it away, Pashmina," Maggie laughs, lightly tapping her arm and motioning at the cell phone. "Don't you ever take a break?"

Pashmina shakes her head. "I'm trying to sort out a back tax issue for the castle. It's been night and day trouble..."

"That's not the *only* trouble the castle faces," Cadet Monroe says, grimacing at Pashmina. "If you'd allocate more funds to security perhaps we wouldn't have a *murderer* running loose about the grounds." Cadet Monroe is still in his uniform, a serious scowl on his face as he pushes his stew around in its bowl. I can't help but notice he seems to direct the comment about a murderer toward Maggie, who seems to lean back in her seat as if she's trying to hide behind Pashmina.

Chef Renauld glances at Cadet Monroe, clearing her throat with all the commitment of an earnest child standing up to a bully on the playground. "Cadet Monroe," she says so loudly that half the table looks up. "While we're on the topic, how *is* your investigation proceeding?"

The room quiets as everyone leans in to hear what Monroe has to say.

"It's proceeding with great haste," Cadet Monroe says in a matter-of-fact way. "Going quite well, actually. We've made some impressive strides."

"By all means," Chef Renauld says, motioning around the table. "Share with us what you know. If there's a murderer among us, I for one would like to be made aware so I can lock my door at the proper hour." The smile at the edge of Chef's mouth tells me she doesn't believe for a minute that someone in this room killed Phillipe.

Unless she's the murderer and she's playing cat and mouse with Cadet Monroe, I think. If that's the case, Chef has the bravery of a lion. She must be confident she's committed the act in such a way it could never be traced back to her.

"I'm unable to share details of an ongoing investigation," Cadet Monroe says with an air of self importance. "But I can assure you, we have some very promising suspects..." He offers a pointed look at Maggie, who shudders, slinking down in her chair.

The Chef scoffs. "That doesn't *sound* very promising," she says. "I'm not sure I believe you have any suspects at all."

Cadet Monroe slams his spoon back down into his bowl just a little too hard. "I'll have you know we've made *excellent* strides. The King and Queen are most pleased with our work. In fact, just this week while going through Phillipe's emails, we found a communication that provides a motive to our key suspect." He looks again at Maggie, whose mouth drops open.

"What motive could there be for such a terrible act?" Chef says innocently, practically fluttering her eyelashes.

"It appears Phillipe tried to get this person fired," Cadet Monroe smiles. Mutters issue around the table as private conversations breakout around the room, no doubt debating who could have had such an altercation with Phillipe. Cadet Monroe dabs at his lips with his napkin, pleased to have proven his prowess as a detective. "Maggie, would you like to comment on this recent development?" The Cadet smiles at Maggie, his teeth gleaming under the lights.

"I—" Maggie stammers. "No, I'd rather not."

The Cadet nods, then puts a hand to his head, as if he's just remembering something. "Wait a moment... if I recall, weren't you nearly fired last year?" More murmurs flood the room as the group realizes what the Cadet is implying. "Strange coincidence, don't you think? Now, if you'll excuse me. I have much to attend to. It shouldn't be long until an arrest is made." He locks eyes with Maggie. "Just tying up a few loose ends." He stands, leaving the table and exiting the room. Side conversations break out, and it's impossible not to feel all eyes on Maggie, who looks like she might be sick. If she was hoping to keep her status as a potential suspect under wraps, that cat is out of the bag now.

Chef seems oblivious to it all, instead delighting in making the Cadet leave the room. "There is nothing more fun than playing with a silly man, no?" Chef says to me, elbowing me in the arm. She stretches, then stands. "I believe we need dessert. I'll attend to the kitchen." She gets up, allowing me to scoot closer to Maggie, who's now found herself alone at the end of the table.

"Are you okay?" I ask Maggie, who's turned white as a sheet. All the blood has drained from her face, and she's staring at the table like she wishes she could disappear into the wood. "Rebecca, I—" she stammers, then reduces her voice to a whisper so no one else can hear. "Last year, Phillipe and I had a disagreement about scheduling, and he sent some emails to the Duke trying to have me fired."

"Why would he do that? You're amazing."

"I was still getting used to the job and we butted heads over the timing of the building. I had so much on my plate and was still learning." She puts her head in her hands. "I honestly forgot about it because the Duke just let it go. He said he knew I was trying my best. And Phillipe eventually saw how much I cared about the place and we all just moved on. I can't believe it's coming back to bite me *now*. And after tonight, everybody knows. They all think I'm a murderer."

"No they don't!" I say. "Not everyone thinks that."

As if to prove my point, Joe approaches, shaking out his golden mane before standing on his back legs and putting both of his front paws on Maggie's knees. He licks her face with a big, determined swing of his tongue, and for a second her whole head disappears. When she reemerges, her face is covered in Joe's saliva. She wipes it down with her napkin. "Thanks, Joe, that was really helpful. At least I still have one friend."

"He can tell you're upset," I say. "And you have *two* friends. I'm not going anywhere."

"Rebecca, what if—" She shivers. "What if I go to prison because of this? Cadet Monroe has a motive now. Things in Monrovia don't work the same way they do in America, especially when it comes to the Royal Family. They're allowed to hold their own internal trials of justice. If he convinces the King and Queen I did it..."

"He *won't*," I say, more determined than ever to solve the case. "We're going to figure out who did it before Cadet Monroe knows what hit him."

And I mean it.

CHAPTER
Eighteen

BY THE TIME Joe and I manage to calm Maggie down, dessert has been finished, and most of the table has been vacated. Tired staff retire to their individual apartments, their bellies full and spirits high despite Cadet Monroe's outburst. With great care, Chef Renauld and I manage to send Maggie off to bed in a calm, relaxed state. An offer of tea in a to-go cup and a freshly-baked croissant from the Chef seems to help, along with the promise of curling up in bed to watch her favorite TV show. I make a mental note to check on her first thing tomorrow morning.

Now that most of the room has cleared out, Joe and I scan the room for any sign of Douglas the Groundskeeper. His chair is empty, nothing but a discarded napkin sitting on its surface. It must have dropped off his lap as he exited. Dirty dishes are stacked in the middle of the table, a series of wax candles burning down, their flames flickering in the night. A few members of Chef Renauld's team start to clear the table, striped aprons covering their uniforms. One of them moves to clear Douglas's spot, her hand reaching out to take the discarded napkin from his seat.

"I'll take that!" I say too loudly.

She backs up at the sound of my voice. "You want... this used paper napkin?" she asks, holding the napkin out to me by its edge.

"I do," I answer, grabbing it. "It's important to recycle. A big deal where I'm from. I'd like to personally supervise its discarding so I can ensure it goes in the right bin."

The woman's eyes widen as she walks away, but she doesn't ask further questions. As soon as she's out of sight and finished clearing the table, I hold the Groundskeeper's used napkin out to Joe, bending down to his level. He's laying on the floor, completely stuffed from the meal of potatoes and beef that Chef prepared especially for him. He opens up one eye, looking at me warily.

"Joe," I say holding out the napkin. "It's time to get to work."

Joe groans, lifting his head with much effort. His eyes seem to ask me, "Do we have to?"

"Yes, we do have to," I tell him. "Now," I hold the napkin in front of his face. "Go find."

Joe doesn't move. Instead, he lets his head plop back down onto the floor, rolling over to show me his stomach in hope of a scratch. His round belly sticks outward, his golden fur coating a round ball. It's as if he wants me to understand how full he is.

"*Joe*," I insist, rolling him back over into his normal "down" position. It takes all my strength to flip him over, because he weighs more than I do. I crouch beside him, scratching his ears. "This is why the monks sent you to me. You're a ferocious guardian beast. Time to act like it."

Joe lets out an audible sigh, like he can't believe he's burdened with a human as obnoxious as I am. I hold out the napkin again, issuing the command: "Go find."

There's a pause as Joe considers his options, then, he reluctantly sniffs the napkin. He spends a good minute thoroughly examining it with his nose, starting at the top and working his way down to the bottom. When he's finally got the scent, he stands, nose to the ground, allowing his sense of smell to follow the trail.

He leads me out of the dining room toward the main hall-way, then through the front doors and out into the courtyard. The night is crisp, and the brisk air makes me pull my sweater tighter around my shoulders. "Good boy, Joe," I encourage as he leads me across the courtyard toward the castle. We pass the castle's back entrance, heading toward a part of the grounds I've never explored before. Joe stops at a little brown gate that's waist-high and attached to a fence of the same size. He pauses, glancing over his shoulder as if to say, "What are you waiting for?"

I open the gate for him and Joe continues following the scent, his nose low to the ground. Together, we stride across a wet, muddy patch of earth that looks incredibly ordinary, except for the construction of a small path of pavers cutting through the space. We stop at the edge of a cluster of trees, all of them overgrown and untamed. Joe looks over his shoulder at me then pushes his way into the uncultivated land, and I wonder for a moment if he's taking me on a wild goose chase. Still, past experience has taught me to trust Joe's nose, so I follow him into the wooded area, ducking low beneath a branch.

We proceed into the cluster of trees, hopping over logs, our feet crunching on the ground as we step over piles of leaves. A second glance at the ground tells me someone else has come this way recently— bootprints are pressed into the dirt, and from the looks of it, they belong to someone with much bigger feet than me.

We duck underneath another low-hanging branch and suddenly we've entered a clearing unlike anything I've ever seen. The land is flat and even, each section tilled in such a way that small rows have been cut into the soil. The land is broken up into various sections, each labeled with a small, wooden sign. We move closer to one of the signs, bending down to examine it. It reads "Strawberries." A little further down the path, another sign reads, "Melons." Raised platforms covered in mesh create stand-up herb gardens, chives and basil growing within. In the distance, there's two structures: a small greenhouse, and a little log cabin. The cabin has a small, wrap-around porch, and based on the size, probably isn't bigger than a single room. Smoke emanates from its chimney.

Just then, I sense a figure behind me. I whirl around, revealing: Douglas, the Groundskeeper.

He's holding a rake in his hand, a yellow slicker covering his typical denim overalls. A bucket hat protects his head from the light mist that clings to the evening air, and his cheeks are a hazy shade of red. They puff out as he scolds me;

"Whaddaya think you're doing here lass?" His voice comes out in a thick, Scottish brogue.

"I—" My mind scrambles, looking for an excuse. "We were touring the castle. We wanted to see the parts we'd never been to on the grounds and we got lost." Beside me, Joe arranges himself in a sit position, an innocent expression on his face. We both know we're lying, and we're working too hard to cover it up.

"Hmmph," Douglas huffs. "Well don't go tellin' the rest of the staff about it. We finally found a place that's away from the targets. We'd like to keep it that way?"

"We?" I ask, unsure what Douglas means.

"The Chef and me," he says, exasperated. "Got right tired of the construction makin' us move our garden all the time. You have any idea what it takes to replant? So, we built our own little paradise right here, on the other side of the trees." He holds his arms open, motioning around the landscape. "The land around the castle goes on for acres. Nobody comes out this way. It's trouble to walk so far to harvest for meals, but Chef is nothing if not a perfectionist."

"So, you moved all the fresh produce and herbs far enough away that you wouldn't have to worry about the building?"

"That's what I said," he confirms, looking at me like I'm thick.

"That means the tomatoes back at the castle..." I think out-loud, putting the story together in my mind. "Chef didn't even need them anymore."

Douglas shrugs. He points at a patch of ground a few yards away. A sign marks the area: tomatoes. "She's been harvesting these for weeks," he says. "These are a better hybrid anyway. The ones at the castle are what's left over from the *last* garden they destroyed."

"Does Chef seem... *happy* with the new garden? I mean, was she still angry at Phillipe?"

Douglas stares at me, then lets out a deep, hearty laugh. "Chef? Angry? Lass, that woman doesn't have the time to hold a grudge. A force of nature she is. She hits a bump in the road and finds her way around. She barely thought of Phillipe once the new garden was established. Right smart woman she is." The admiration in his voice makes me wonder if his feelings for Chef exceed professional boundaries.

I glance at the cabin behind him, smoke emerging from it's chimney. "Do you live there?" I ask, surprised.

Douglas nods.

"You don't want to stay in the new staff quarters?"

"I've been livin' there fifteen years," he says, pointing a finger at the cabin. "Why would I move into some fancy new apartment when I got everything I need right here. Nature. Quiet. Privacy..." He offers Joe and me a pointed look, "When I'm *lucky.*"

"Right," I laugh, sensing that it's time for us to exit. I grab Joe's leash and pull him away from a patch of strawberries, where he's trying to lift a leg. "Sorry, we'll just be on our way."

"Good thing," he nods. "He's already peed on the cucumber patch."

"Sorry about that!" I shout, pulling Joe with me back toward the trees.

"It's faster to go up the road," Douglas calls after us, but Joe's already leading me back through the woods. We move as fast as we can, driven by the fact that for all I know, I was just alone with a murderer in a place where no one could hear me call for help.

Finally, we're back in the castle courtyard, moving toward the safety of the staff quarters at breakneck speed. I don't know if Douglas is innocent or not, but if what he says is true, Chef wasn't holding a grudge against Phillipe. Maybe the fact he was strangled by a tomato vine was more about opportunity than personal attack.

But what about Douglas? His voice betrayed a care for Chef. Is it possible he felt Phillipe disrespected her, and chose to act on a grudge himself?

Later— after washing the mud off both of our hands, feet, and paws— Joe and I snuggle into our warm bed, pulling the blankets tightly over us. Thoughts of who killed Phillipe buzz in my ears, until Joe's stable, heavy snores finally coax me to sleep.

CHAPTER
Nineteen

THE NEXT MORNING, Maggie, Joe, and I meet outside the castle's towering facade, waiting for Enrique to pick us up and take us to town. We've made plans to camp out at a charming bookstore and cafe in Atwood village, where we can sort through Phillipe's letters to Monique away from prying eyes. It's early, and the sun is just rising on the horizon.

"Enrique's going to hate me for asking him to drive us at this hour, but it's the only way we'll have true privacy," Maggie says, hiking her purse up on her shoulder. She's put herself together after the debacle at last night's dinner, and re-emerged as the best version of herself. She's wearing a cute, plaid dress, her hair neatly tucked back in her finest braids.

"Good," I agree. "We're going to get to the bottom of this, Maggie. I've printed out the photos we took of the letters, and they're all in my bag. We'll read through each one carefully and see if Phillippe mentioned anything suspicious that could —" Before I can finish my sentence, Joe lets out a deep, throaty bark.

I turn around to see what he's barking at, and find Pashmina behind us, her eyes blurry. She's wearing the same blazer she wore at dinner last night, and her hair is pushed to one side in a frizzy bun. Her cell phone is in her hand, and she's carrying a file in the other.

"Pashmina?" Maggie says, horrified. "You look terrible."

"Thanks," Pashmina says, her tone biting. "That's what everyone wants to hear when they've worked an all-nighter. I so appreciate your support, Maggie."

"Uhm," Maggie tries again. "I meant to say, you look terrible but your natural beauty still shines through. It's almost a fashion statement. You're like a combination of CEO and cave-woman."

"*Not better,*" I hiss at Maggie, deciding to take over the conversation. "Pashmina, what were you doing all night?"

"I was in the library going over the castle financials," she says, sighing. "It was all so much easier, with the old Duke. Now—" She looks away, her eyes watering. "Everything will be fine. I just need to keep going over the numbers. That's where the answers are. They're in the numbers. Numbers don't lie." She glances down at Joe like she's just noticed he's there. He's sitting a few feet in front of her, staring up at her with a blank expression. "Have fun going into town with the *animal,*" Pashmina says. Apparently, she's not a dog person. Joe cocks his head at her as if to say "what's your problem, lady?" Without answering, Pashmina stiffens, then makes her way across the courtyard, barely able to walk a straight line.

"We need to send someone to check on her," Maggie sighs, quickly typing an email on her cell phone. "Maybe I'll have Tracey stop by today to talk to Pashmina about fitness and work-life balance."

Yes, I think to myself sarcastically, *a lecture on doing yoga and drinking smoothies is exactly what she needs right now.*

"I think she just needs a good night's sleep," I say. Just then, Enrique's SUV with the tinted window pulls up, the wheels crunching over gravel.

"Someone ordered a ride?" He smiles at us through the

driver's side window, which is rolled down. "You're giving me heartburn with these early mornings, Maggie."

"Sorry," she says, opening the door to the backseat and hopping into the car. "Next time we'll walk, but today we're on a schedule."

"No kidding," Enrique says, revving the engine and driving us down the long road that leads over the castle bridge.

It occurs to me that Enrique is also on our suspect list. I've never taken him seriously as a possible suspect only because we were with him most of the day that the murder occurred. But then again, there was a thirty minute gap between when Enrique brought us back to the castle and Phillipe's murder. If Cadet Monroe listed him as a suspect, I owe it to all of us to vet Enrique's possible involvement.

"Has Cadet Monroe interviewed you about the murder?" I ask Enrique, trying to sound casual. I'm hoping I can frame the conversation as one that's more about Cadet Monroe than Enrique himself.

"That guy?" Enrique snorts, glancing out the window at the lush landscape rolling by. "He's always been a character. The Royal Family allowing him to lead this investigation just confirms what I already thought about the state of things."

"And what's that?" I ask, leaning forward in my chair.

"Look, what the Duke is trying to do with the Castle is admirable. But there's a reason things worked in the past. Everybody knew what was expected of them. When you try to change things, you get unrest. And idiots like Monroe are brought in to counteract the change. The Duke should have left well enough alone. But who am I to have such thoughts? I retire in two years anyway." He looks over his shoulder at me, pulling down the sun visor to reveal a photo that's clipped on the edge. It's of Enrique and a woman with curly hair, standing in front of the beach. "My wife and I are headed to the South of France. We bought a little cottage out there. Just counting down the days."

"Did you tell the Cadet you had an alibi?" I ask, glancing at Maggie. "He seems to like accusing the wrong people."

"I told him as soon as I dropped the two of you off, I took the SUV back to the garage for maintenance. All the guys that worked there can vouch for me." Enrique laughs as a row of stone buildings with red tile roofs appears outside the windows, indicating we've reached Atwood Village. "Funny thing about Cadet Monroe investigating the murder is that he has the most to gain from it, doesn't he?"

The tires screech as Enrique pulls up to the village center, parking just outside a fountain that features angels spitting water toward the sky.

"What do you mean by that?" Maggie asks, her cheeks flushing with excitement. I know what she's thinking: it would be so satisfying if Cadet Monroe were arrested as a suspect after all he's put her through.

"Well, the Cadet's wanted to move up in the ranks for as long as I've known him," Enrique shrugs. "The two of us have been here the longest, and he's part of the old guard if you will. His goal has always been to get promoted to protecting the King and Queen themselves. They've never taken him seriously, given his lowly status guarding the Duke of a rural country. But now... it seems this new development has given him the opportunity to prove his worth, hasn't it?"

Enrique's words run on repeat through my ears, like a song I can't shake. *Cadet Monroe has the most to gain from the murder.*

"Thank you again for the ride," I say, jumping out of the van and whistling for Joe to follow. His enormous body hops down to the ground with ease, his paws leaving massive prints on the dusty cobblestone.

"I'll come get you at the end of the day?" He asks. Maggie confirms our return trip, and with that, Enrique takes off, leaving us to our own devices in the quaint village of Atwood.

We saunter down the cobblestone street toward the combination bookstore and cafe Maggie chose, noting the beauty of the village. Ivy winds up pastel storefronts, and the air feels crisp and clean.

"Is it terrible that I'm kind of hoping Cadet Monroe—" Maggie starts to say.

"Don't finish the sentence," I sigh, shaking my head. "It's too beautiful a thought. Don't jinx it by saying it out loud. But yes, it would be poetic."

"Satisfying," Maggie agrees.

Cadet Monroe has the most to gain from Phillipe's murder. I can't deny it— the image of Cadet Monroe being hauled away in handcuffs brings me a sick satisfaction. I'm eager to read Phillipe's letters and now, a huge piece of me is hoping Cadet Monroe will be implicated in some way.

All we need is proof. I peak down at my tote bag where the stack of letters waits, full of promise and foreboding.

CHAPTER

Twenty

THE COMBINATION BOOKSTORE and cafe Maggie has introduced me to is called *Cafe de Flore*, and it's the most adorable place I've ever been to in my life. We step inside, and the walls are lined with shelves, carrying books of every genre. There's a section for cozy mysteries, one for romance, and another for fantasy. A display near the front door offers a "blind date with a book," in which the owner's favorite reads are wrapped in brown paper and twine, with nothing but a description on the front and some pressed flowers decorating the wrapping. That's another thing that makes this place special:

The proprietor is a fan of flowers, and they're everywhere. All around the store, flowers of different kinds weave their way up the walls from within their ceramic pots. Fresh bouquets are for sale in stands outside the entrance. There's a counter at the front where guests can order drinks inspired by floral flavor: a lavender latte, a rose cappuccino, a hibiscus iced tea. Even the pastries are decorated with little icing-artwork in the shape of petals and leaves.

Maggie, Joe, and I order at the counter, and the cashier gives us a placard to put on our table with the order name,

"Petunia" written on it. A set of French doors at the back of the store opens to an expansive outdoor patio that's almost bigger than the shop itself. Tall shrubs create a private oasis, blocking off the patio from the world outside. A set of fountains bubble, the peaceful sound of running water creating a calming atmosphere. Metal cafe tables sit beneath striped umbrellas, offering shade. The wicker chairs circling the tables are padded and soft, featuring arm rests and fluffy pillows that invite a visitor to sit for as long as they'd like. The three of us grab the biggest table that's unoccupied, and Joe settles down on the brick patio, letting his legs sprawl out behind him.

"This place is amazing," I tell Maggie as our food arrives. I've ordered a Bruschetta-style, open-faced breakfast sandwich, and it's gorgeous. Runny egg sits on top of burrata cheese, the freshest tomato I've ever had cushioning its fall. "Their food might be as good as Chef Renauld's," I say, mouth full.

"Don't tell Chef that!" Maggie laughs, taking another bite of her lemon-ricotta pancake. She rips off a piece and tosses it to Joe, who opens his mouth and snaps it up in a single chomp. A big bowl of water sits beside him, along with some chopped ham on top of an egg.

"You're sure no one will see us here?" I ask Maggie, glancing around the patio. We've arrived early enough that the place is pretty quiet, except for a couple of lovebirds sitting at a table across from us. They're holding hands, and I wonder if they're tourists on their honeymoon. For a moment the couple makes me think of Travis, and there's a tight feeling in my chest.

"We're too early," Maggie answers. "Life in Atwood Village doesn't usually start until ten in the morning. We live by a different pace than you do in America."

"Great," I say, nodding, my eyes still glancing at the couple across from us. I wonder what it would have been like to come here with Travis? Maggie seems to notice that I'm distracted, because she clears her throat.

"Did you hear anything else from *l'enorme connard*?" Maggie asks, using the nickname she's reserved for Travis alone, *"l'enorme connard,"* which I've learned means "the enormous asshole." I've told her about Travis's constant text messages and reach outs, which haven't stopped since the first night he wrote me.

"He called me three times last night," I say. "I didn't pick up. He's left voicemail after voicemail. He says he made a huge mistake and that we were dating for so long he just panicked. I haven't called him back because..." I pause for a second, thinking. "Well, I guess because I don't know what to say."

"Tell him he's the worst and that he should regret what he did for the rest of his life in private like a normal person," Maggie shrugs. She sighs, leaning into a sliver of sunshine that's managed to evade our umbrella. "Thank goodness you'd *never* get back with that guy."

I don't say anything, because if I'm being honest, there's a part of me that *has* wondered if I could ever forgive Travis. It's tempting to imagine that we could just pick up where we left off. And— if Castle Atwood goes underwater— walking back into my old life would offer a prickly sort of comfort, like wrapping an old blanket around my shoulders.

The idea of Castle Atwood no longer existing makes my breath catch in my throat, and I shake away the feeling. I don't have time to waste thinking about Travis. I need to deal with the problem in front of me and try to save the place I've grown to love.

"Let's solve this murder," I tell Maggie, reaching into my bag and removing printed pages of the photographs we took of Phillipe's letters. We divide them into two stacks, pens and highlighters at the ready to mark anything that might be relevant to Phillipe's demise.

An hour flies by, and as I read the letters, I can't help but feel a growing connection to Phillipe. When I met him, I could tell he was a sensitive man, but his letters to Monique reveal a depth of romance any woman would yearn for. In his letters, Phillipe addresses what he loves about Monique, and none of it is physical. This is a man who really *knows* the woman he's come to adore. He talks about the tone of her laughter, and how it reminds him of the carefree feeling of summer. He brings up his adoration of her love of reading, and in one letter, even mentions that he's purchased a book she recommended that's about two lovers living in different cities during the fall of the Roman Empire. As their love affair changes with time, the length of the letters shortens, but the depth of feeling remains. The shorter letters are brief and rather banal— like a post-it note one might leave for a partner on the kitchen counter— but there's a curt sweetness to them unlike anything I ever shared with Travis. One such short letter reads, simply:

> I missed you at breakfast.
> Today is a beautiful day, because I know
> I will see you tonight.
> Be well, mi amore.
> — P.

I'm three-quarters of the way through the stack of letters when I start to wonder if I've placed too much hope in them. I was sure my gut instinct would prove to be correct and the letters would reveal some motivation for Phillipe's murder, but so far, they're just ordinary love letters. Incredibly romantic, yes, but still ordinary. Just when I'm thinking there's no way the letters will lead to anything helpful in solving the murder, I stop at one that catches my eye. It reads:

My darling,

Today was long, and I am tired. I discovered something most terrible about 'la personne grise.' I must have a difficult conversation with the Duke tomorrow, but perhaps will give this person an opportunity to explain before I do. Pray for, Mi amore. I will tell you all tomorrow night at dinner.

Yours,

— P.

I check the date on the letter, and sure enough, it was sent just one day before Phillipe's murder. It occurs to me that whatever terrible thing Phillipe discovered might have given someone motivation to kill him in order to keep him quiet. And the difficult conversation he'd planned with the Duke must have never happened, as I'm sure the Duke would have mentioned it. Unless, of course, he was involved in Phillipe's murder himself.

"Maggie," I say, looking up at her. She's got her head in one hand and a letter in the other. "I think I found something," I tell her.

She sits up with a start, an excited expression lighting up her face. "Oh thank goodness," she says. "Because all I'm reading is a long list on Monique's best qualities." She shivers, goose pimples scattering across her arms. "I'm starting to feel creepy reading so much about their relationship."

"Look at this," I tell her, passing her the letter. "It's the last letter Phillipe ever sent, and he sent it the night before he was killed."

"*La personne grise?*" She reads aloud. "The grey person? I wonder what that means?"

"I don't know," I shake my head. "But whoever this grey person is, maybe they killed Phillipe to keep him quiet. He says he discovered 'something terrible' and was going to tell the Duke. And he was planning to tell Monique the next evening but he never got the chance to tell her because—"

"He was strangled by a tomato vine," Maggie nods. "This could be it."

"It could," I agree, "But we have to figure out who the grey person is."

"We're on to something," Maggie says, taking a sip of her lavender latte. "I can feel it."

———

Later, Joe, Maggie and I walk back to the town center, where we wait for Enrique to pick us up at the fountain. Now that we have a lead on the case, the air feels lighter and more fragrant, imbibed with a hopeful freshness I haven't felt in a long time. While we wait for Enrique, we stop at a pop-up at the marketplace that marks the town center. Stands sell local goods, from homemade jewelry to fresh honey, candles, and vegetables. Maggie informs me that the marketplace is held every couple of weeks, and that any resident of Atwood Village can sign up to sell their wares.

I peruse the tents, stopping to look at a table of candles, when something else catches my eye. The stand next to the one I'm shopping at is selling newspapers and gossip magazines, including one that features a picture of Castle Atwood on the front.

"Oh no," I murmur, pulling Joe away from the candle he's sniffing and toward the rack of gossip magazines. My hand shakes a little as I pull down the magazine with the picture of Castle Atwood on the front.

The headline reads:

"CHIEF ARCHITECT MURDERED AT CASTLE ATWOOD: Is the Duke of Death to blame?"

"Did you find anything?" Maggie says, her voice chipper as she appears by my side holding a shopping bag.

"Just this," I tell her, passing her the magazine.

"Oh my gosh," Maggie squeals, dropping her shopping bag to remove her cell phone from her purse. "I have to call our publicist."

"You can call, but I think it's safe to say the cat is out of the bag." Maggie looks at me, confused. "What cat?" She says.

"It's an American expression," I laugh at her. "It means there's no putting the genie back in the bottle."

"What genie?" She asks.

Mercifully, Enrique's black town car pulls into the middle of the town square, parking near the fountains. I give up on the expressions and pull Maggie and Joe toward the car, unable to ignore the looks the villagers are shooting our way. They recognize the car as castle property and now, the castle is a place of death.

If we don't solve this murder soon, they're going to shut the place down.

I have to find the grey person.

CHAPTER
Twenty~One

MAGGIE SPENDS the entire drive home trying to do damage control. She makes call after call, first to Castle Atwood's publicist, then to the public relations department that's in charge of the entire royal family. Next, she reaches out to the head of household for the King and Queen— her counterpart— and attempts to get a feel for whether or not this has impacted the castle's future. From the sound of it, the King and Queen aren't happy with the press.

When we reach Castle Atwood, Maggie excuses herself for a meeting with the Duke. "He might have ideas about how we can fix this," she says, sounding as if she's trying to reassure herself more than me. "The Duke is smart. He's strategic. We'll come up with something to buy us more time before they shut us down. It's going to be okay," she squeezes my hand before running up the castle steps.

Joe and I head for the animal courtyard together, completing our nightly care for each creature. We make sure the sheep are brought back into the barn for the night— something Joe helps with. He's become quite the herding dog during our time here. Next, we feed Alfredo the giraffe. I've managed to get him on a mostly plant-based diet, but he does still insist on a serving of pasta noodles whenever we engage in training exercises. In exchange for the snack, I've already taught him to come when called, and lay down when asked. Thanks to an agreement with Chef Renauld, I have home-made noodles stored in a small fridge in the barn, and am able to spend a few minutes working on behaviors with Alfredo. For awhile he seemed annoyed at my visits, but now, he looks forward to the woman bearing pasta.

Next, I feed the horses their nightly apples, and brush their manes in calm, even movements. A few of them started out as averse to touch, but I've already managed to persuade them to let me groom them. Soon, they'll be open to a rider, although I'll proceed with baby steps.

As I work with the animals, my mind races over what I've learned so far about Phillipe's murder. The suspects race through my mind:

There's me, and I know I'm not guilty, which means one suspect down. Then there's Maggie, who I know wouldn't hurt a fly. There's Enrique, the driver, who has an alibi. Tracey, the fitness expert, who also has an alibi at the time of the murder. Next we have Monique, who appears to have been so in love with Phillipe, I can't imagine she'd have hurt him. Next on the list is Pashmina, who's so wrapped up in the castle finances she hardly seems like a person who has time to commit murder. There's Douglas, the groundskeeper, who still strikes me as a mystery, albeit one without a motivation to kill. After Douglas, there's Chef Renauld, who was mad at Phillipe for making her move her crops, but who appeared to have remedied it with the secret garden I found. It's hard to imagine her as a murderer. Finally, we have Cadet Monroe— who has gained the most from the tragedy— and the Duke himself, who can't be the murderer because...

Why can't he be the murderer Rebecca? I ask myself, afraid of the answer.

He can't be the murderer because he's too charming.

It's a bad answer, but it's the only one I have at the moment. Everything in me wants the Duke to be all that he appears to be. But I've been wrong before. And I can't help but wonder if it's possible Phillipe found something secret in the Duke's files. They were working so closely together.

I inhale sharply, dropping the apple in my hand as a terrible thought hits me.

The grey Person.

Among many of the Duke's charming features sits the fact that he has dashing salt and pepper hair. It's one of his most noticeable features. The Duke has gone grey in the George Clooney kind of way that can make the right kind of man so very appealing. His impressive head of hair is a mix of silvers and greys spread throughout a darker, cool-toned shade of asphalt. Even his beard displays the same variety of grey tones.

What if the Duke is the Grey Person? It would make sense. If Phillipe discovered something terrible about the Duke, he would never dare mention him by name in a letter, and would instead cover it up by using a pseudonym like "the grey person." What if when Phillipe said he was going to talk to the Duke the next day, it wasn't with the intention of reporting a problem, but rather— with the intention of *confronting* the Duke himself?

A shiver runs down my spine. Could the Duke... be a killer??

———

Dinner is held in the staff dining room, and Chef has cooked up an incredible meal of chicken cordon bleu with a side of string beans and some kind of raspberry jelly that's so fresh I feel as if I've picked the berries off the vine myself. Maggie and I have taken a seat at the end of the table, not just for privacy, but so that Joe has more room to spread out on the ground without bumping anyone's legs.

"The Duke and I have a plan to buy some time," Maggie says. She reaches into her purse and slides a flyer toward me. It reads, "CASTLE ATWOOD OPEN HOUSE: FREE TO THE PUBLIC." A description underneath promises visitors a tour of the grounds, food stands, games for children, and animal interactions.

"You're holding an event that's open to the public?" I ask, surprised. "I thought we were waiting until the castle was ready—"

"The Duke thinks some positive press might help turn all of this around," Maggie answers, taking a bite of her chicken. "He feels like if he can't prove his idea now, he might never get the chance. We're hoping holding an open house will show everyone in Monrovia that there's nothing to fear in change. The entire village of Atwood is invited, along with press from around the country. This is our chance to change the impression of the castle. Show that it's not... uh—"

"A murder castle?" I say helpfully.

"Right!" Maggie exclaims. "It's not a murder castle, it's a place where everyone works together and the Royal Family can finally give back to the community. I'm meeting with the entire staff to talk action items. We are all going to be busy the next few weeks, I'm afraid. You too, unfortunately..."

Maggie spends the next twenty minutes walking me through everything I need to accomplish before the public open house. The Duke's number one concern is making sure the animals are comfortable, so he's requested a write-up from me about the best ways to keep them away from any noise, including how much of a radius is necessary for their protection. Maggie also asks if there's any animal that might be comfortable visiting with the public.

"Ace would be great," I tell her. "Hawks are predators so they're not stressed out as easily as prey animals. And as you and I both know— he's already learned a few helpful behaviors." I wink at Maggie and she smirks back. It's fun, having our own private secret.

Once Maggie and I are solid on the plan, she heads down the table to meet with another staff member, bumping into Pashmina along the way.

"Pashmina!" She exclaims. "We need to roundtable tonight about making sure the funds are in place for this." Maggie passes Pashmina one of the flyers, and the blood drains from Pashmina's face. She adjusts the collar on the pale, charcoal suit she always wears, pushing her ashen hair back.

"You can't be serious," Pashmina says, mouth dropping open. "Maggie, we're already tight. There's no way the budget allows for this—"

"The Duke okayed it himself," Maggie counters.

"This is out of control!" Pashmina's voice raises, and other members of the staff look up at her in surprise. "You two always want more from me and I'm a financial officer, not a magician."

"This is the plan," Maggie shrugs. "We have to make it happen."

"We'll see about that!" Pashmina says, marching out of the room with cheeks so red I'm surprised her head didn't explode.

On her heels, Cadet Monroe rises from the table— a dinner napkin still tucked into his shirt— and stops Maggie in her tracks, holding out his hand to receive a flyer. "Give it here," he says, and Maggie passes it to him, her eyes betraying a hint of fear.

"Hmmph," he snorts. "Did you and the Duke think to run this past security?"

"If you have a problem with it, I guess you can call the King and Queen," Maggie says, puffing out her chest. "The Duke spoke to them on the phone, and they agreed to allow the public open house."

Cadet Monroe leans in, raising a finger to Maggie's face. "Perhaps they'll feel differently when I submit my final conclusion as to who committed the murder. I'll be sending it for their consideration any day now. Don't think I'm not onto you."

With that, he exits, leaving a flushed Maggie in his wake.

CHAPTER
Twenty~Two

AFTER A HOT BATH in our glorious soaker tub, and a quick read of a book by the fireplace in our apartment, Joe and I retire to bed. His warm, plush body sprawls out next to me. I'm on the grounds of a beautiful castle in a custom apartment with my every need attended to, and yet— I can't relax. Sleep evades me as I consider the facts of the case.

Please don't let the Duke be the killer, I think.

For some reason, the idea of the Duke— or Jack, as I've come to know him— being a killer makes my heart sink. It's not that I imagine anything could ever happen between us, but simply the fact that he was restoring my confidence in the idea that there are attractive, interesting men in the world who don't sleep with the dog-sitter.

I try flipping to my other side, but sleep still doesn't come. Finally, I sit up in bed and turn to Joe.

"Do you feel like a nighttime romp?" I ask him.

He lifts his head and arches his golden eyebrows at me in a gesture that definitely means "no." Still, at my urging, Joe gets down off the bed and follows me into the kitchen, where I grab a handful of cheese to lure him outside. I like to tell myself that Joe is agreeing to go for a walk because of his deep love for me, but I know the cheese has something to do with it as well.

The night air sits cold and even on my shoulders, my breath interrupting the quiet in a steamy trail of heat. I'm in silk pajamas, the blanket I usually leave at the end of my bed now wrapped around my shoulders like a shawl. We cross the castle courtyard— Joe stopping briefly to chase a squirrel — then make our way up the castle's back entrance, heading down the stone hallway toward the library. The castle is quiet this late at night, and the flickering chandeliers scattered down the hallway light our steps in a golden, even glow.

There's a small piece of me that hopes the Duke will be at the library, studying among the books. I can't ask him directly about the murder— "Excuse me, but did you strangle Phillipe with a tomato vine?" isn't a question you can ask royalty— but maybe he'll be able to quell my fears some other way. His presence alone might be enough to remind me that there's a reason I trusted him upon our first meeting.

The doors to the library offer an eager squeak as we push them open. The crackle of the fireplace greets us, inviting us forward. The library feels warmer than the hallway thanks to the fireplace's roaring flames, and I let the blanket I'm wearing drop from my shoulders as Joe and I enter the space. It smells of books and burning wood, and immediately makes me feel at home.

Then, I see him. The Duke— Jack— is in the library after all, just as I hoped he would be. He's seated at one of the long, wooden tables, and his head is resting on an open book, his arms splayed out across the table.

He must have fallen asleep while reading, I smile to myself. The Duke's tendency toward literature strikes me as nerdy in the most charming kind of way. Joe and I approach him on tip-toe, careful not to frighten him awake. When we reach the table, I notice a teacup beside him, the amber liquid within still releasing tiny spirals of steam. He must have filled the cup recently, considering its still warm. Across the table—splayed out in front of him— are all sorts of plans for the upcoming open house. There's a drawing of the grounds in the Duke's own hand, showing where he plans each attraction to be stationed. A list of food vendors is beside it, and brainstorming bubble of possible games for children, including corn-hole.

"See, Joe," I bend down to scratch Joe's chin, whispering in his ear. "He can't be a murderer. He's thinking of games for children."

Joe lets out a whimper, and for the first time, I notice his tail is tucked between his legs. He runs past me, moving around to the other side of the Duke and reaching up to sniff his face. I move behind the Duke's chair to get a better look at what Joe has already noticed:

The Duke isn't sleeping. He's passed out.

His chest isn't rising and falling, but instead, sits motionless. As I move closer toward his face, I notice his lips are blue, and there's a puddle of spit that's come up from his mouth.

Horrified, I step back, gasping as my hand rises to my mouth. Before I know it, I'm screaming into the night as loud as my lungs will allow me to scream.

"Joe," I shout. "Get help!" I make one hand into a fist and put it over my other hand, demonstrating the sign language word for "help," which Joe and I have adopted as our training signal for "emergency." Joe's been trained to find the nearest human and bring them back to me anytime he sees this signal.

Joe runs to the library doors at lightning-speed, making a right at the hallway and heading toward the main castle stairs. His deep, throaty bark echoes through the chamber, carrying into the library and probably up the stairs, undoubtedly waking up every one within a ten mile radius. For a moment, my heart swells with gratitude, so proud that

Joe didn't ask for cheese in order to perform this important task.

Then, my attention returns to the Duke. I pull him off the chair, which takes great effort because he weighs so much more than I do. Still, I manage to wrestle him to the floor, where I lay him out flat on the ground. I straddle him, placing one of my hands over the other and hovering both above his chest. I don't feel a pulse and he doesn't appear to breathing, so I start compressions, counting to the beat of the song "stayin' alive." I don't dare stop or look up, even when I hear voices in the library. Shoes come into focus at the edge of my vision— slippers, to be exact— but I don't look up. My only focus is saving Jack's life.

"Call the Doctor!" I hear a familiar voice shout. It's Maggie.

A pair of boots exits the edge of my vision, and only minutes later, someone in a robe appears.

"Rebecca, you can stop. It's okay now, they're here," Maggie says, her gentle hand touching the edge of my shoulder. But I don't stop, because I'm frozen, a record stuck on repeat, my hands continuing CPR of their own accord. A team of men come in and lift the duke away from me onto a stretcher, and I finally sit back on my heels. A warm, wet feeling coats my face. It's Joe, giving me a kiss on my cheek. He sits beside me, and Maggie leans down to our level.

She pulls me closer to her and hugs me tight. "It's going to be okay," she says, more to herself than to me. "No matter what, it's going to be okay."

But nothing feels okay at all.

CHAPTER
Twenty~Three

"HE'S BREATHING," the Doctor says, a stethoscope around his neck. "Your compressions likely saved the Duke's life. It's a miracle you found him in time."

Maggie, Joe, and I are corralled in one of the castle's many sitting rooms, heavy drapes framing a set of french doors. The three of us take up an entire couch, our bodies pushed together. Across from us sits Doctor Frey— a plump, bearded man who apparently lives in the village and leapt out of bed as soon as he got the call.

Sprinkled throughout the room are the few members of the staff who've been informed of the situation. Cadet Monroe is there, a striking set of purple, silk pajamas looking particularly glamorous on his lithe frame. Seeing Cadet Monroe in his pajamas makes me want to vomit, but I hold the feeling back as we've got bigger problems at the moment. Against the far wall is Chef Renauld, her hands shaking, face as pale as a ghost. Next to the Chef is Pashmina in a pale nightgown, her hair arranged in a bun, arms crossed.

"We need to inform the police," Maggie says, trembling a little. "This is a direct attack on the Duke's life—"

"The Duke has requested we keep this information among

our household only," Cadet Monroe scoffs. Even though he's not wearing his traditional fluffy hat, I can still picture it on his stupid head, almost as if it's a part of him. "The Duke fears calling the Police would create more concern about safety in the village, interfering with the public open house you two have decided to hold... *against* my security recommendations."

"The Duke just wants to show the community what we're all about—" Maggie starts to say before Cadet Monroe interrupts her.

"Hogwash!" The Cadet snarls. "The Duke has been *beguiled* by his head of household assistant, who is likely behind these attacks to begin with..."

"How can you possibly still think that?!" Maggie exclaims.

"What were you doing in the castle so late at night?" The Cadet counters.

"I was going for a walk outside because I couldn't sleep due to... stress," Maggie confesses. I get the impression the stress she's referencing is Cadet Monroe's own investigation, although she'd never admit it in his presence. "And I heard Joe barking."

"It's true," I tell him, raising a weak arm into the air. "Joe and I went to the library and the Duke was alone when we found him. I sent Joe to bark for help."

Joe offers a bark in response as if to prove the theory we were presenting.

"And what about you?" Cadet Monroe turns to Chef Renauld. "Why were you in the castle?"

"The Duke asked for a cup of tea," the Chef says, looking bewildered. "Usually the request goes to night staff but I gave them all the evening off because there's so much to do for the open house this weekend. I wanted them to be well-rested. I said I would handle any evening requests myself. I never dreamed a simple cup of tea could—"

"We're having the tea tested," Cadet Monroe answers,

pausing as if for effect. "The Doctor believes the Duke was poisoned."

Maggie gasps, putting a hand over her mouth as if the idea is too awful to believe. Beside her, Joe whimpers.

"The tea never left my sight," the Chef says, shaking her head. "I brought it to him personally an hour ago."

"We should cancel the open house," Pashmina adds. She's been so quiet during this entire escapade I almost forgot she was there. "Besides the fact we don't have the funds, it's not safe to have so many people around the Duke. Not now that there's been an attempt made on his life."

"And what were you doing at the castle so late?" Cadet Monroe asks, arching an eyebrow.

Pashmina shrugs, impatient at the question. "I was going over our finances, yet again. The Duke has left me no time to get the funds in place for an event that occurs in a few days. There are vendors to pay. Insurance to buy. It's quite a hassle, as you can imagine."

"Did you see anyone else on the premises?"

"No," Pashmina says as if that fact should be obvious. "I was in the office of finance, not the library. I had just left out the castle's main exit. It was Joe's bark that made me turn around, just like Maggie."

There's a tense pause as Cadet Monroe considers our stories, looking around the room as if each and every one of us was a murderer. For a moment I expect him to haul us all off to jail, but instead he throws his hands in the air.

"If the Duke wants this kept a secret, then a secret it will be," he says. "You are all forbidden from telling anyone about the events of this evening."

"I really think we should cancel the open house," Pashmina says, pushing the issue. "We can't keep going this way. Tight on money. A murderer on the loose. Surely the King and Queen will shut us down if we don't fix this. Have they said anything of the sort to you, about shutting us down?" There's a desperate edge to her voice that stands out to me, although I'm not sure why. I file the information away in case it becomes important later. Maybe Pashmina can't afford to lose this job.

"It *would* be nice to have more time to consider the food options," Chef Renauld said wistfully. I notice the small lines around her eyes, and am convinced she hasn't been sleeping, either. It seems the events at the castle have taken a toll on us all.

"I've voiced the same opinion to the King and Queen, but they appear determined to allow the Duke to have his way with the event," Cadet Monroe says. "They indicated to me it's his last stand, if you will. Whether we like it or not, the Duke is piloting this ship, and I am instructed to honor his wishes. And tonight, he had only two requests. First, that the open house continue."

Pashmina groaned, leaning against the wall for support, clutching a notebook tight in her hands. Beside me, Maggie let out a sigh of relief.

"And, second," Cadet Monroe continued, "he wished to speak to the woman who saved his life." He stares at me, skepticism etched in his scowl. "Rebecca Orange. He'd like to speak to *you*."

CHAPTER
Twenty~Four

I OPEN THE HEAVY, wooden door to the Duke's bedroom suite, with Joe on my heel. The Duke's bedroom is located on the second floor of the castle, and entering it feels like I'm breaking a rule. But when we make it inside, I'm surprised at how normal the space is. It's not inspired by ancient architecture or the French rococo era like the rest of the castle. Instead, the Duke has constructed a modern, Scandinavian suite. There's a walk- in closet in one corner, a TV on the far wall, and an enormous bed settled between two sleek end-tables where an alarm clock sits.

"I'm sorry to greet you this way," the Duke waves at me from the bed. He's smiling, and— I'm relieved to see— breathing. The fact that he's okay almost makes me choke up, but I clear my throat and push the feeling down.

"We're relieved to see you're alive," I tell him, walking toward an arm chair across from the bed and taking a seat. "You gave us quite the scare."

"Hi, buddy," the Duke says to Joe. Before I can stop him, Joe gathers all his strength and takes a giant leap from the floor onto the bed, settling in next to the Duke in order to get pets.

"Joe, *down*," I hiss, but Joe ignores me. Instead, he allows Jack to scratch his ear, leaning into his new friend. "I'm so sorry! I'll get him—"

"Nonsense," the Duke waves a hand in the air. "Although I do find it quite funny that we've hired an expert animal trainer whose own dog doesn't always listen to her."

"Joe has his own ways," I say. "Even the Tibetan monks didn't have enough patience for him. I think I'm practically worthy of Sainthood for what I've accomplished with Joe."

"Remind me to call the Vatican," Jack smiles, then leans forward somberly. "Seriously, I have their number."

I can't help but laugh. It's a relief to see the Duke back in action. Still, it's awkward that I'm in his bedroom. I shift in the chair, wishing he would get to the point. He was the one who wanted to see me, after all. The Duke seems to notice my discomfort, because he cuts right to the chase.

"I only wanted to thank you," he says, his voice earnest. "Rebecca, you saved me."

"Joe had a lot to do with it, too," I tell him.

"Of course he did," Jack nods. "But I think we both know I'd be gone without you. I'm sorry to meet you like this, but they've forbidden me from leaving my bed for at least a day."

"And you, of course, won't listen to them," I tease him. "I hear you're already committed to going forward with the open house."

"Yes," he says, his eyes darkening. "Rebecca, I don't think we can *stop* the open house now. Isn't it interesting that whoever did this to me chose to make their move just after I announced my attention to open the castle to the public?"

"What are you saying?" I ask him, heart racing. It seems as if I'm not the only one who's been secretly trying to solve Phillipe's murder.

"I've been poking around," the Duke admits. "Looking into Phillipe's death. And it occurs to me now that whoever killed Phillipe might have wanted to stop our progress on the new direction I'm taking the castle. Phillipe was a core part of the plan. He was familiar with all of our goals in the building process— our only architect. First him, now me. I wonder if the person behind all of this simply doesn't want the castle to serve as a model of a new way of doing things. Maybe they don't want us to open the grounds to the public, to be more transparent."

My mind races. The Duke might be right. Everything he's saying makes sense. The murders occurred in conjunction with the Duke's announcement of his plans. And Phillipe played a key role in those plans.

"Whoever they are, they're getting more desperate," he says, leaning back on the pillow behind him and stretching his arms out with a grimace. "Attacking me through my tea was a low blow."

"Why are you telling me all this?" I ask him, eyes wide. "You shouldn't be alone with anyone. Someone on your staff could be the killer!"

"I'm telling you because I trust you, Rebecca," he blinks at me, as if it's obvious. "I have a good instinct for people. I see how you are with Joe and well— even before you saved my life tonight, I was quite glad to have you here." He pauses, almost like he's questioning if he should say more. "And I was wondering if, once I'm well again, you would let me host a dinner to thank you for saving my life. Just the two of us. It will have to be here at the castle, because anywhere else leads to stories in the magazines, I'm afraid."

Is he asking me out? I've made the mistake of dating someone I work with once before, and it's not one I'm eager to make again. Still, I try not to read too much into it. The Duke is an amazing person who treats his staff like they're family. That's all this is. And if that's the case, it's safe to agree to a simple dinner, isn't it?

"Dinner sounds wonderful," I tell him. A nervous tingle runs down my spine, but I choose to ignore it. I came to

Monrovia seeking new adventures, and I'm not going to miss out on a private dinner with my boss— the Duke— whose life I just saved only because lingering memories of Travis make me afraid to seize the moment. Life is too short to let an experience with one man define every experience that comes after.

"Joe can come too," he says, scratching Joe's stomach. "I'll make sure there's a prime rib waiting for him."

"As long as someone tests the tea," I think out loud, glancing at him when I realize I might have said too much. "Oh my gosh," I say, wanting to apologize right away. "Was that too soon?"

The Duke laughs, throwing his arms in the air. "Not too soon at all. After all, humor is what gets us through the worst of times, is it not?"

"It is for Joe and me," I say, whistling for Joe to jump off the bed. For once, he listens to me, and I reach into my pocket to reward him with a piece of cheese. "If we didn't have a sense of humor, we'd both be toast by now. We're glad you're okay," I tell the Duke. "We'll see you soon."

"See you soon," the Duke smiles at me as Joe and I make our way out of the room, shutting the door behind us with a gentle, easing sound. As the door shuts behind me, I can't help but notice the way my heart skips a beat.

Even if it's not a date, this castle is magical. Monrovia is a place that's brought me back to life when I could've fallen into a deep pit of despair. I think about the friends I've made here, and how at home I'm starting to feel in my little apartment.

And it all could be ripped away, if I can't find the murderer.

I march down the steps, Joe at my flank, thinking about what the Duke suggested: the murderer doesn't want the castle to succeed.

Twenty-Five

THE NEXT DAY, Maggie and I return to *Cafe de Flore* in the Village Atwood to discuss everything that's happened. Flowers lace up the trellis near our outdoor table, the sound of bubbling fountains coaxing Joe into a gentle nap at my feet. Birds tweet overhead, building their nests in the awning that extends across the first third of the patio. Maggie sips her cappuccino, wiping the foam from her mouth.

"In the hallway this morning I overheard Cadet Monroe saying they got the results back on the tea," Maggie whispers, leaning in to talk to me over her Belgian waffle and raspberry jam. She cuts into it, taking a bite, talking with her mouth full because this food is too good to leave unattended. "The pathologist said it was definitely poisoned. The Duke is lucky to be alive."

"Did he say what type of poison?" I ask, cutting my breakfast sandwich in half. It's a delicious melting puzzle of warm cheddar cheese on top of a slice of ham and egg, positioned carefully under a homemade English muffin smothered in Hollandaise sauce. The egg runs across my plate and a little bit drips onto the floor. Joe promptly wakes from his sleep, licking it up with his tongue as if it were a treat meant just for him.

"Some kind of household cleaner," Maggie shrugs. "They said just a couple ounces more and he would have been done for."

"Cleaner?" I ask, shaking my head. "That brings me back to Monique, although she just doesn't strike me as a killer. She has no motivation, and given that she was sincerely in love with Phillipe, didn't want him dead."

"No evidence of a quarrel, between them," Maggie agrees. "We need a culprit with a motive."

"Oh!" I exclaim, remembering I haven't filled Maggie in on the Duke's theory. "The Duke told me last night he thinks the killer might be someone who wants to stop the castle's plans from moving forward."

Maggie takes this in, dipping her Belgian waffle straight into the shallow dish of jam, rubbing it in for good measure. "Enrique has always been against the Duke's new direction," Maggie thinks out-loud. "And Cadet Monroe is a traditional monarchist."

"What about Chef Renauld?" I ask. "She had access to the tea. Phillipe was strangled with a tomato vine. As much as I like her, both attacks seem to have a connection to Chef..."

"It doesn't look good," Maggie nods. "But I just don't think Chef is capable of something like that. Besides, she doesn't match Phillipe's description of 'the grey person.'"

"True," I agree with her. "So the killer needs to be someone who wants to stop the Duke's plans for the castle," I hold up my index finger, counting through our qualifications for the murderer. "They also need to be someone who fits the description of the grey person." I put another finger in the air, making my second point. "And they need to have had access to both Phillipe and the Duke at the time the attempts were made." I hold three fingers up in the air.

"We're close," Maggie says. "If we could just figure out

who the grey person is, we'd know more. I'll ask around today while I'm working. See if I can subtly get some more dirt from the staff."

We pack up our stuff, removing notebooks and pens from the table before grabbing Joe's leash and heading back into the store portion of *Cafe de Flore*. We take a minute to browse the aisles of books, and I even end up buying one to read later. It's a romance novel about a waitress who falls in love with a Prince before she even knows he's royal. As I'm at the register checking out, Maggie gives me a knowing glance. "I bet the Duke is very grateful you saved his life," she says, smiling at me as if she knows a secret I'm not in on. I don't say anything, but tuck the book in my bag, alongside a dried and pressed rose that the store's owner gives me with my purchase.

"Leave it on your bed-stand and it will help you follow your heart," the owner says to me as she hands me the flower.

After a brief walk in the sunshine, we make our way back to the castle and go our separate ways, both of us consumed by preparations for the upcoming open house, which begins tomorrow morning. Despite the short notice given to the staff, everyone at Castle Atwood is doing their best to deliver on the Duke's idea. As I walk through the main hallway, I wave at Monique, who has the entire cleaning staff scrubbing the space from top to bottom. "Good morning, Rebecca," she chirps at me while wiping down a wall. "And hello to you, Joe," she slips Joe a cookie from her pocket, and I feel a rush of guilt that I was— only ten minutes earlier— once again wondering if she might be the murderer. I glance at the cleaning fluid she's using to wash the wall. It's a light amber-colored disinfectant I've never seen before. It would blend in perfectly with tea.

"Monique," I ask her, staring at the cleaning product. "Was all your cleaning supplies where you left it this morning? Had anything been moved around since yesterday?"

Monique looks at me in surprise. "No," she says, shaking her head. "We store everything in the cabinet down the hall, across from the executive offices. It was all where we left it." She pauses, concern etched in her eyes. "Why? Did something happen?"

"Nothing," I assure her. "Maggie just asked me to make sure everyone has what they need to prepare for tomorrow."

With that, Joe and I make our way through the French doors that lead to the courtyard. As we step out onto the sprawling grounds, we're both shocked at what's before us. In just a matters of hours, the staff has managed to transform the grounds entirely. Large, pop-up tents designate certain areas for eating and others for games. A corn-hole set-up takes up the far Western corner, and it's positioned next to a croquet playing field, complete with wickets, balls, and hoops. Signs send visitors in a multitude of directions, telling them which way to head for various activities.

At the back of the courtyard I notice Douglas— the groundskeeper— using a rake to collect leaves at the edge of a tent. Joe runs toward him and jumps in the pile of red and yellow chaparral, much to Douglas' chagrin. I grab Joe by the collar and scoop up the leaves he's displaced, pouring them into the trashcan next to Douglas. "Sorry about that," I say.

"Not to worry," Douglas shrugs, although there's a gruff tone to his voice that tells me he's annoyed with us.

"What do you think about all this?" I motion around at the castle courtyard. "Do you like the idea of the Duke opening up the castle to the public?"

"To be frank," Douglas sighs. "I think it's about time. Royalty has to adapt don't they? This new generation wants more and maybe they're right."

No motivation for murder, then, I think. Joe and I swiftly wish Douglas well before making our way toward the animal courtyard. On our way there, we cross paths with Tracey, wearing work-out clothes as usual, her hair in a ponytail and a smoothie in her hand. "Rebecca!" She waves at me. "Isn't it looking great?" She motions at the transformed castle grounds. "Tomorrow I'm offering a free mat pilates class to anyone who comes to the open house. You should sign up!"

"Definitely will," I assure her, even though I have no desire to endure another training session with Tracey.

When Joe and I arrive at the animal courtyard, we take a moment to feed the giraffe, Alfredo, and practice some training behaviors with him for tomorrow. Joe sits peacefully under a tree while I work with Alfredo, practicing the actions I've been teaching him for "down" and "come." By the end of the training session, Alfredo proves that he can "come" to me when called, and lay down on the ground when asked. In my proposal to the Duke, I've suggested allowing the public to view Alfredo and the roaming sheep throughout the day, given that "ungulates"— or hoofed animals— don't seem to mind human visitors too much. Hoofed animals tend to do well in petting zoos because the presence of a human doesn't cause them undue stress. I'm not planning on demonstrating Alfredo's behaviors to the visitors, but it's still important to have a couple basic commands mastered to ensure his safety. If the crowds become too much for Alfredo, I'll easily be able to call him back into the barn with the "come" command.

Alfredo leans down, nudging my hand with his nose to ask for another treat. "You like these as much as pasta, don't you bud?"

The giraffe gives me a side-eyed glance from overhead, as if to say he couldn't like *anything* more than pasta.

Later, I head for the barn to check on Ace in the aviary. He jumps on my gloved-arm without a moment's hesitation, and I can't help but feel satisfied with the quick progress we've made. In no time at all, the giant hawk has learned to trust me. Together, we make a great team.

Ace balances on the leather glove as I carry him out to the courtyard, where we rehearse our flying routine. To help the demonstration, I put a dollar bill in Joe's mouth and signal for him to run away from me, then sit. He does, crouching down with the bill still in his mouth. At my signal, Ace launches into the air, spreading his wings wide. He circles Joe, then dives down and grabs the bill out of his mouth, bringing it back to me with confidence and ease. Tomorrow at the demonstration, we'll ask an audience member to hold up a piece of Monrovian currency in bill-form, and Ace will snap it out of the volunteer's hand, enabling me to joke that I've just gotten richer. It's a bit we performed often with our birds at the Safari Park, and it always gets a laugh. It also provides a segue to ask for donations, and given that the Duke is committed to making sure all animals at the castle are part of conservation and rehabilitation efforts, donations may be something we can accept in the future.

After serving Ace dinner and tucking him in for the night, Joe and I head back to the castle for a meal of our own, energized from doing what we both love most, hopes for tomorrow still swimming in our eyes.

I CAN ALWAYS COUNT on Chef Renauld to serve up something delicious and tonight is no exception. The staff dining room is packed— after a long day working to prepare for tomorrow's open house, not a single team member wanted to miss Chef Renauld's latest creation. Flickering candles light the table, and the Chef has decorated the space with center-pieces down the line. Each one features a collection of field flowers in orange and yellow, surrounded by greenery creating an elegant bouquet.

I glance down at the meal in front of me. An elegant ravioli dish sits before me, spinach folded inside hand-pressed pasta, all of it smothered in a lemon-cream-sage sauce. As a side, Chef has cooked up a crisp salad featuring pears and apples on top of a bed of lettuce, a sweet, fruity glaze poured over the concoction. A glass of red wine pairs perfectly with the entire dish, offering a slightly dry, fruity flavor profile.

Beside me, Maggie takes a bite of her ravioli, letting out a deep groan. "Ughhh this is so good. Food this good should be illegal," she says.

"Those noises you're making are going to get us in trouble," I laugh. "You're giving me *When Harry Met Sally* vibes."

"I can't help it," Maggie answers. "Chef is so good at what she does." She leans in, whispering. "Please tell me she's not the murderer. If she is, maybe we should keep it to ourselves so she can keep cooking."

"If we keep it to ourselves, you might go to prison," I remind Maggie.

She points her fork at the pasta dish. "For this ravioli? Worth it. Lock me up." She reaches down to move Joe's tail out of her lap. He's on the floor underneath the table, eating a plate of his own that was cooked up by Chef, just for him. It's a custom dish of chicken liver on a bed of cranberries and spinach. The description didn't appeal to me personally, but judging by the way Joe is scarfing down the food, Chef is also a great cook in Dog-world.

"I asked around about the grey person today and what Phillipe might have met, but wasn't able to get anything out of anybody except Monique," Maggie whispers, looking down the table at the rest of the staff. "Everyone is here tonight. Isn't that interesting?"

I follow her gaze down the table, clocking our potential suspects. Enrique has his driver's hat beside him, and is talking animatedly to Monique, who's still in her housekeeper's uniform and is on her second glass of wine. Douglas is at the end of the table, and he's changed out of his groundskeeper uniform into a crisp, white shirt. I'm surprised to see him at dinner— he usually eats alone in his little cabin at the edge of the castle grounds. Tonight, he's not only joined us all, but dressed up for the occasion. He's seated next to Chef, who's eating her own food, still wearing her white Chef's outfit. The two of them laugh, apparently sharing a secret joke about the spinach.

Tracey is on the other side of the table, and for once, she's not drinking a smoothie. Instead, she eats her ravioli with enthusiasm. I hear her say something about carbo-loading for tomorrow. Beside her, Pashmina is on her cell phone, completely ignoring the incredible food in front of her. Next to Pashmina is Cadet Monroe, who pushes his food around his plate, looking unimpressed. Nothing makes the man smile.

"What did Monique say about the grey person?" I ask Maggie, my heart quickening in my chest.

"I didn't ask her directly," Maggie whispers, taking a sip of her wine. "I didn't want her to figure out we looked at the letters. I told her Phillipe had mumbled something to me about a problem with *the grey person* right before he died, and wondered if she knew what it meant."

"And?"

"She was surprised I knew anything about it," Maggie shrugs. "But she told me Phillipe had been having issues getting the equipment he needed to build, and was always complaining about not being able to hire enough help. She wondered if the *grey person* conflict had something to do with that." Maggie takes a bite of her salad. "She was planning to talk to him about it the next night, but then, you know..."

"He was murdered," I nod.

"It's okay," Maggie tells me, patting my knee with her hand. She can see I'm bothered by not yet having an answer as to who killed Phillipe. I feel like we're close to something — like the answer is on the tip of my tongue— but I just can't make the pieces fit together. "We have a big day tomorrow. Let's put the case aside and try to have fun? If Cadet Monroe hasn't arrested me yet, I'm still a free woman." She gives me a weak smile. "If the open house is a success and leads to good press, maybe we'll save the castle another way."

After dinner, I head back to my suite, still unable to shake the feeling I'm missing something obvious. Joe curls up on the couch with a bone, but I head straight for my cork-board of suspects, looking at the images of everyone who might be the killer.

What am I missing? I think to myself, trying to pull the pieces apart. I review the alibis and motivations under each suspect, hoping something will click, but nothing does.

Just then, a dinging noise echoes from my cell phone. I've left it on the kitchen counter. I reach for it, and the name on the front sends a rush through my veins. I hate that he still does that to me after so many years together.

TRAVIS

I really wish you would answer me. I have something important to tell you.

I hesitate, looking at his name on the screen. In a moment of weakness, I wonder what harm it would be to write him back. If the castle is failing, I might be forced to head home anyway. But even then, I know— deep down— that Travis doesn't deserve me.

I pause, considering, then put the phone facedown on the table. As if he knows I've read the message and am choosing to ignore him, Travis sends another text, and the phone buzzes again.

TRAVIS

A second chance. Just think about it. People can change.

People can change? I think to myself, wanting to throw my phone across the room. The fact that Travis thought he needed to tell me as much is mind-shattering. Obviously, people can change. *He* changed into someone who sleeps with the dog- walker.

Later, Joe and I head for bed, his fluffy, golden fur pressed against my stomach. I push aside thoughts of Travis, and the open house tomorrow. Whether it's solving the murder or helping the open house succeed, I hope I can save Castle

Atwood. In the midst of doubt and fear, there's one thing I know for certain: this place is special.

I glance at my bedside table, where I've left the flower I was given by the shop owner at *Cafe de Flore*. The dried rose is perched at table's edge, poised to help me follow my heart, just as the shop owner said. As I close my eyes, thoughts of the staff, and the Monrovian countryside, and memories of the sweet scent of Chef's cooking lure me to sleep.

IT'S the day of the open house, and the castle grounds are buzzing. Joe and I wake up early, heading straight to the staff dining area for a fancy coffee from the gold espresso machine the Duke had delivered as a "thank-you" to staff for all their hard work over the past few days. The machine is almost three feet tall, and it looks like something from Willy Wonka's Chocolate Factory, all levers and buttons. A simple pull of one of its metal arms creates a perfect coffee, laced with chocolate syrup and topped with foam. There's a hissing sound as the coffee pours into my mug and steam releases from the top of the machine.

"He's almost as tall as the coffee-maker," someone says behind me. I reverse, discovering Douglas, the groundskeeper, his hair tousled. He's wearing a loose t-shirt, and pajama pants. It looks like he just woke up. He nods toward Joe, who's seated at my feet, tail-wagging.

"Oh!" I laugh. "Yeah, Joe's my shadow, if my shadow were bigger than me." I pause, wondering what Douglas is doing here so early. "I thought you stayed in the cabin, not the staff quarters?" I ask.

Douglas arches an eyebrow at me. "I do. But when I hear

there's a special espresso machine available for staff, it's worth the morning walk." He winks at me, then takes a sip of his coffee, heading toward the front doors to the courtyard. "Lots to do today!" He calls over his shoulder at me as he exits. Joe and I peer out the windows to watch him crossing grassy lawn, whistling a happy tune as his figure disappears into the morning fog.

It's not long until the entire staff shows up for their coffee, and the room is buzzing with activity. Tracey leads a small group of staffers in what she calls a "morning stretch," offering a fifteen minute calming yoga session to anyone who wants to enter the day in a "relaxed state of mind." Chef Renauld and her assistants cross in and out of the kitchen, carrying platters of food in catering trays. In the courtyard, Monique arranges trashcans in a line, planning to disperse them across the grounds in the most strategic formation to encourage proper disposal of garbage.

"It's amazing how we can all come together to do something great, isn't it?" Maggie asks me, flipping one of her braids over her shoulder. She checks a clipboard in her hands, going down a list of action items. "Monique's made sure there's plenty of trash receptacles. I'm really hoping our guests are respectful. And then there's the food— the private vendors are arriving in an hour, and Chef is handling everything in-house. How are you doing with the animals?" She asks, turning to me. "You've rehearsed the presentation, right? Is there anything else you need?"

Suddenly, I feel butterflies in my stomach. I've done hundreds of animal interactions over years of working at the Safari Park, but the idea of being in front of a group of people never fails to make me nervous. "We're ready," I tell her, swallowing hard. "Ace did great yesterday. His flight was gorgeous. Even Alfredo learned a couple tricks. Plus, I have the best assistant." I bend down to scratch Joe's head.

"I knew you'd be prepared," Maggie smiles at me kindly,

checking something off her list. "Perfect. We'll send the guests your way twice today. The first show will be at 11a.m., the second at 2p.m. That should give the animals time to unwind, and give you a chance to have lunch. And maybe play a round of corn-hole with me."

"Please," I tell her, adding in a whisper, "Otherwise Tracey will make me take her pilates class."

Maggie laughs. "Stick with me. No pilates required."

Before I know it, the morning is over and it's time to let in the public. The staff gathers at the entrance to the castle grounds, where a tall, iron gate protects the property. Behind the gates is a long line of guests from not just Atwood Village, but the entire country of Monrovia. Joe sits at my feet, looking out at the crowd of people on the other side of the gate. He barks at a familiar face.

"Is that the owner of the *Cafe de Flore*?" I whisper to Maggie, recognizing the villagers. "And that man over there owns the bakery! They've all come."

"It's a great turn out," Maggie agrees. "My estimate says we'll have over a thousand people today! And the press showed, thank goodness..."

She motions at a cluster of visitors off to the side of the line, wearing badges and carrying cameras. Cadet Monroe stands in front of them all, accompanied by two security guards, his arms crossed. He wears a displeased expression.

Suddenly, the cameras flash, and murmurs arise from the crowd. The reporters throw their hands in the air, their voices creating one overwhelming sound. The Duke has arrived.

He waves at the crowd, but stops to greet the staff, smiling at each one of us. Then, he steps up to a platform that Maggie rigged with a microphone.

"Thank you all for joining us today," he says into the microphone, his voice blasting across the courtyard. "Today marks a new day at Castle Atwood. I've always felt that the truth about a monarchy is that it belongs to the people— and, as such, a monarchy should *serve* the people. Today, we welcome you to a new version of Castle Atwood that exists to serve."

Jack makes a sweeping motion with his arms and the iron gates open. The public floods in, scattering across the grounds. Reporters descend upon the Duke, all of them asking for a statement. Various questions are called out one after the other:

"Can we get a comment on the recent murder of a staff member—"

"How is the castle able to remain financially stable—"

"Defining the use of tax payers funds—"

The Duke waves them away. "My dear friends!" He laughs at the press, and I can't help but think the word "friends" is meant ironically. "There will be time for questions later. For now, enjoy the day, and let the event speak for itself."

He steps down from the platform and heads toward the courtyard. As the Duke passes Joe and I, he stops to whisper in my ear:

"I hope you'll give me the honor of beating you at a game of Croquet?"

"I'll give you the honor of *losing* a game of croquet," I say. Jack smirks at me.

"It's a deal," he agrees. Then, he disappears into the crowd. Visitors flood the courtyard like ants on a picnic, and all at once, the castle grounds are busier than I've ever seen them.

"It's time," Maggie squeals, jumping up and down. "I've got so much to take care of. I need to make sure the food tents are operating properly, and check-in on Chef. And— oh!" Her face flushes as if she's just remembered something. "I'm giving the first castle tour in fifteen minutes!" She squeezes me arm. "If you need *anything* let me know. Your animal inter-action is going to go perfectly."

Maggie takes off, leaving Joe and I alone to navigate the crowd. I check my watch. Our show doesn't start for an hour, so Joe and I have time to mingle and enjoy before the presentation. We weave our way through the courtyard, watching as visitors enjoy Monrovian spiced-popcorn and games of cornhole.

"Pretty amazing, isn't it bud?" I expect Joe to give me his usual bark in response, but when I look down— he's gone.

"Joe?" I call, my heart pounding. He never leaves my side, unless of course, there's steak to be had. Or cheese. Or hot dogs. "*Joe?!*" I shout again. "Speak!"

A throaty, familiar bark echoes from a nearby tent, and I run toward it, discovering Joe. He's standing in front of someone I know very well, growling, keeping the person pushed to the back of the tent. I have to blink, because I'm sure what I'm seeing is in my imagination. But it's not a dream. He's really here.

"Travis?"

Twenty-Eight

TRAVIS STARES BACK AT ME, his hands up in the air like he's about to be arrested.

"I know," he says, trying to step toward me. Joe growls at him, keeping him in place. "I flew here on a red eye. At least let me explain."

"*Explain?*" I shout. A few visitors walking by stare at me, and I take a breath, hoping I can keep my voice down and not cause a scene. "You show up here without any notice— just bombarding your way into *my* new life—"

"I missed you," Travis says, a pained look in his eyes. "We'd been together so long. I panicked. I made a huge mistake." He looks down at Joe, who's still in a guarding stance. "Did you teach Joe to hate me?"

"No," I tell him. "You did that all on your own."

"He's never growled at me before," Travis says sadly.

"Well, that was before you abandoned him, broke *my* heart, shattered what we had, cost me my job, and left me for the dog- walker. I can't *imagine* why he's not your biggest fan anymore."

"Can you call him off?"

I think about giving Joe the order to attack, but instead, I issue a low whistle. Joe obeys the command, and returns to my side, but he doesn't stop looking at Travis with a skeptical gaze.

"What are you doing here?" I ask. "Whatever you came to say—"

"I came to ask you for a second chance. Not over the phone, but in person." He steps toward me, taking my hand in his. "It was a fourteen hour flight, but I came here because what we had is worth fighting for. I broke it. Give me the chance to fix it."

My mouth searches for words, but doesn't find any. Instead, I say the only thing that pops into my head. "I'm working," I tell him honestly. "I'm doing an animal presentation. I can't unpack all of this right now."

"That's fine," he says, pretending to understand despite the disappointment that flashes across his face. "Maybe tonight when the event is over you'll let me take you to dinner. We can talk then."

"Maybe," I agree. Then, I motion for Joe to follow me, and the two of us exit the tent together like we're walking out of a dream.

CHAPTER
Twenty-Nine

I TRY to shake off my run-in with Travis and focus on my job at the open house. In front of me is a large crowd of people, waiting to see the animal presentation I'm hosting. A low wooden fence keeps the crowd separate from the animal courtyard that's situated in front of the barn. Visitors stare at me, their mouths open in awe. A small child holding a bucket of popcorn points at me. An older gentleman leans on his cane, a serene smile crossing his face.

Meanwhile, I'm standing next to Alfredo the giraffe, a single one of his legs taller than my entire body.

"Here at the castle, all of our animals are rescues who wouldn't survive in the wild," I tell the crowd, adjusting the mini- microphone that's clipped to my shirt. At first I was nervous, but now, my years of experience at the Safari Park come rushing back to me. "Alfredo here was found alone on the African plains when he was just a calf."

A little girl in the front row who can't be a day over ten raises her hand, pushing her hair out of her face.

"Yes?" I say, nodding at her encouragingly.

"Why was he out there all alone?" She says, her brow furrowing in concern.

"Because there are people out there who hunt these animals for money," I tell her. "And our job today is to show you all how wonderful they are in the hopes you'll help our conservation efforts." I smile at her. "Conservation means 'keeping these animals safe.' Every one of you can help protect these incredible species."

"Why do people do bad things for money?" The little girl asks again, her eyes welling up.

Uh-oh, I think. *I don't have the answers to cure this kid's existential dread.*

"Umm," I say, concerned we're heading for a full meltdown. "That's a complicated question. Before I answer it, let's show you what Alfredo can do."

I turn to Alfredo making an "up" signal with my hands. Right on cue, he kicks his front legs into the air like a horse bucking in reverse. The crowd cheers. As a reward, I throw Alfredo a piece of dried pasta with some melted cheese on top. The cheese has made a sticky mess in the fanny pack where I keep my treats, but Alfredo has a preference for pasta, so here we are.

"Alright, Alfredo," I say more to the crowd than to the giraffe. "Do you think we should call your best friend, Ace?" After a cue from me in the form of a hand motion, Alfredo bends his neck in a mock-nod. I turn to the audience, throwing my hands up in the air. "Let's all call Ace together! I'm gonna need your help. On the count of three, everyone whistle with me as loud as you can. One, two—"

A chorus of whistles echoes from the crowd. Beside me, Joe spins in a circle, excited by the sounds from the group. He's nothing if not a natural performer, and I never cease to marvel at his love of being in front of a crowd.

I turn toward the barn, where I've left Ace free on his perch. Sure enough, at the sound of the whistles he emerges from the atrium area, his enormous wings flapping in the air. I slip on a leather glove and he lands on my arm with ease, creating a wind to rival any fan. He lands with such force it blows my hair back, and the audience lets out a chorus of "oos" and "aahs."

"Ace is a red-tailed hawk," I tell the group. "Female hawks are typically larger than the male hawks, so Ace here is kind of a little guy compared to ladies out there. They're incredible hunters and can spot prey from 100 feet in the air. Does anyone here want to help me prove it."

A flurry of hands go up in the audience. Everyone wants to volunteer for an interaction with Ace.

Near my feet, Joe lets out a little whine. I follow his gaze, noticing a group of people waving at me. Maggie has come to see the show, and she's giving me a wild wave. Next to her is the Duke, wearing a baseball cap low on his head. He gives me a cheeky grin and a thumbs up, and I can't help but wonder if that hat is meant help him blend in. I notice he's also lost his suit jacket somewhere along the way. Behind them is some of the staff, including Tracey, who's drinking a smoothie, and Enrique, who looks relaxed. I assume the woman beside him is his wife. Further down the line is Chef, standing next to Douglas the Groundskeeper, who's holding a cotton candy. On the outskirts of the group is Pashmina, chewing on her nails and looking glum. She's in her favorite grey suit again.

The woman can't unwind, ever, I think to myself as I stare at Pashmina's tense form. Even on the weekend, I don't think I've ever seen her out of her grey suit.

"Me, me!" A little boy shouts from the back of the crowd. He's probably eight years old, and he looks so desperate to interact with Ace I know there's no way I can choose anyone else.

"This young man right here," I say, pointing at him. "Step on up to the front. Now, do your parents have any cash on them?"

Nearby, his Dad shakes his head. *Uh-oh,* I think, realizing I've backed myself into a corner.

"Uhhh," I glance at the Duke and Maggie, hoping they'll come to my rescue. "Maybe our staff could rustle up some cash?"

"For one of our villagers? Anything!" The Duke says quickly. There's murmurs across the crowd as they realize the man in the baseball cap is actually the Duke. "Perhaps, Pashmina, you could—"

"Yes, fine," Pashmina says icily, reaching into her bag and pulling out a grey wallet. She removes a piece of paper Monrovian currency. I haven't become totally familiar with their exchange rate yet, but I know this particular bill is close to one hundred U.S. dollars. "Will this do?"

The Duke takes the bill from Pashmina and passes it to the young boy, who holds it in his hand like it's something precious.

"Great job!" I say to the boy. "Now hold your arm up in the air like this," I demonstrate the movement for him. "Ace is going to come help make me a little richer. Don't move a muscle, because hawks have been known to confuse ears with money, and I don't want you to lose an ear! Although you have another one, so you'd be alright."

The boy laughs, but looks a little nervous, too. He steps forward and when I can see he's frozen still as a statue, I give Ace the signal. Ace takes off into the air, then swoops low over the boy and grabs the paper money, bringing it right back to me with a graceful return to my gloved hand. The boy's mouth drops open and he gasps in delight.

"Let's get a round of applause for our brave volunteer, and for Ace," I say. The crowd claps. "And, uh, I'll just keep this money," I joke, putting it in my pocket. "A tip from our generous Duke, am I right?"

"Not from me!" Jack shouts, laughing and pointing at Pashmina. "It's a gift from the lady in grey!"

The crowd laughs, but suddenly, my blood runs cold. I stare at Pashmina, wearing her favorite grey suit. It strikes me that I've never noticed her hair is a dirty shade of ashen blonde that, at times, reads quite grey. And her expression is so plain— so unmoved— that her face gives a grey effect. Her expression is always a solid, bored, unhappy grimace. If it were a color, her demeanor would be grey.

The grey person.

My eyes widen. I stare at Maggie, and I can see by her expression that she's reached the same conclusion I have. She stares at Pashmina, a horrified look on her face.

The answer's been in front of us this entire time: Pashmina is the grey person.

Thirty

FOR A MOMENT, I forget that I'm wearing a microphone and standing in front of a crowd. It's as if Pashmina and I are the only two people that exist in the world. Without thinking, I blurt out:

"You're the grey person."

The crowd quiets. Everyone stares as I walk closer to the dividing fence, Ace still on my arm, Alfredo seated in the courtyard, and Joe trailing my feet. "Pashmina, did you fight with Phillipe?"

"I—" Pashmina stammers. "Well, we came to bat over a few things every now and then. The spending of money, for one. But I didn't— I wouldn't—"

"You killed him," I say, more sure of it than I've ever been of anything. "He found out something he wasn't supposed to know and you *killed* him when he confronted you about it." I pause, wondering what it could have been that Phillipe knew. Then, I happen to catch sight of the little girl in the audience who asked questions about Alfredo early in my presentation. I remember what she said:

Why would somebody do something bad for money?

"Money," I nod, pacing back and forth as the picture comes

together. "Before the current Duke took over the castle, you were working for the Earl. The two of you received taxpayers' funds from the Royal Family to take care of castle expenses, and yet, when the current Duke arrived, the castle needed renovations and had fallen into disrepair. Why *was* that Pashmina? Where did the money go?"

Pashmina steps back, looking as if I've slapped her. The Duke stares at her as if he's suddenly realizing what I've realized:

Pashmina killed Phillipe. And she poisoned the Duke.

"You were there that night at the library," the Duke says slowly, piecing it together. "I saw you and I told you about the plans for the open house."

"Yes," Pashmina practically spits. Her eyes light up like fire, angry lines forming between her brows. "*Public.* You and Phillipe needed everything to be public. What ever happened to privacy? What ever happened to dignity?"

"You almost killed me," the Duke says, unable to believe a member of his own staff would do something so terrible.

I glance at Maggie, who's stepped away, cell phone up to her ear. She's speaking in urgent hushed tones, and I'm sure now that she's called security. I only hope I can distract Pashmina long enough to keep her here until they arrive.

"That's why you killed Phillipe," I say, the picture getting clearer. "You gave him such a hard time about the budget that he went back into the castle financial archives to see where the money went before the renovation, and he figured out that you and the old Earl were pocketing it for your personal use. And then— when he tried to confront you, you killed him, didn't you?

"If they'd just left good enough alone it would have been fine!" Pashmina answers, practically pulling out her hair, spit flying in frustration. "But the two of them were so insistent that all our dirty laundry be aired for the world to see—"

"You didn't want the Duke's plans for the castle to go

forward because it would mean transparency," I continue. "The castle's financials for the past ten years would be made public, and the whole world would know what you did. You killed Phillipe to try to slow down the plans for the castle, and then, when the Duke announced the open house, you got desperate—"

Just then, Cadet Monroe appears at back of the crowd in his fluffy hat, three other security officers at his side. The crowd gasps, parting to let them through, and Pashmina stares around the courtyard, looking for any exit. She's boxed in by the Duke and Maggie on one side. On the other side, the villagers stand with their arms crossed, the crowd too dense to make an escape. Finally, she looks at me, glancing over my shoulder at the open courtyard.

It happens so fast I can barely believe what I'm seeing. Pashmina kicks off her heels and runs toward the dividing fence that keeps the animals away from the audience, propelling herself over it like a pro marathon runner leaping past a hurdle. She lands on the grass in front of the fence with a slam, then takes off, breezing past Joe, Ace, and me. She's headed toward the courtyard's back gate. If she reaches it, she'll be able to slip out onto the street and make her escape.

My mind races, and I notice the Alfredo is stationed near the gate, reaching up to a tree branch for a snack. I turn up my microphone and shout as loud as I can, "Alfredo! Sit!"

Alfredo glances at me with a lazy look in his eyes like he'd rather do anything else.

"For pasta!" I shout again. "Sit!"

Just as Pashmina is about to reach the gate, Alfredo decides the action is worth it for a snack and lands on the ground in a heap— directly in front of the back gate. Pashmina skids to a stop as she realizes her exit has been blocked.

"Joe!" I shout. "Sic her!"

There's a loud growl as Joe takes off across the courtyard, rushing toward Pashmina. By now, Cadet Monroe and his men have made it over the fence, but Joe streaks past them all, heading straight for the woman who almost killed his second favorite human, the Duke of Atwood.

Pashmina screams at the sight of Joe's enormous teeth, slobber dripping down his chin. As cute as Tibetan Mastiffs are, attacking and guarding is what they were bred to do. They were made to be terrifying, and right now, Joe is succeeding.

I can't believe I cuddle with him at night, I think, proud of my brave boy. *What an absolutely terrifying creature.*

Joe reaches Pashmina, and just when I'm worried he'll rip her throat out, he jumps on top of her, hitting her in the chest with his front legs and pinning her to the ground. She screams, unable to move with Joe on top of her. He leans down, no doubt preparing to bite her arm, but instead...

... he licks her face. He coats her with kisses from his enormous tongue, ignoring her screaming the entire time.

I've never used the attack command before, and I realize at once that Joe and I have mis-communicated about what "attack" really means.

"Get. Him. Off. Of me!" Pashmina shouts. She tries to push his giant shape off of her without success, her little arms flailing underneath his weight. Just in time, Cadet Monroe and his squad arrive, pulling Pashmina out from underneath the enormous predator I've sent to take her down. I run toward Joe, pulling him away by the collar.

"Bud," I tell him. "You are an absolute failure as a guard dog." I bend down to his level, pushing my nose on top of his soft, golden head. "But a perfect success as a best friend. I love you."

He gives me a giant kiss, and I can tell by the look on his face that he thinks this entire experience was a very fun game meant to bring him pleasure. There's an *awww*-ing sound from the crowd, and I realize I've left my microphone on the entire time. I spin around, smiling and waving at the group.

"That's it folks, thanks for enjoying our totally fictional show! Tell your friends." I rip off the microphone, throwing it toward the ground just as the Duke and Maggie run toward me. They've both jumped the fence, and Maggie has Ace perched on her shoulder. He must have flown away from me in all the chaos, and frankly, I don't blame him.

"Ace!" I shout, concerned.

"He's okay!" Maggie says, trying not to shake. "He, um, flew off your arm and must have remembered me from the day we got the envelopes." She offers a nervous laugh. "He really likes me I guess. I'm just trying not to think about how easy it would be for him to kill me." She gulps. "Were you serious about the thing you said to that kid regarding ears being ripped off?"

"No," I tell her, trying to be reassuring. "But I would worry more about the grip strength of his feet over that. They can hold more than 200 pounds per square inch."

"Uh-huh," Maggie says, looking a little pale.

"You're not afraid of birds, are you Maggie?" The Duke pats her free shoulder in a joking way. It's clear that Maggie is terrified.

"Can you just—" Maggie nods at me and I hold out my arm for Ace to land on my gloved hand again. He removes himself from Maggie's shoulder, circling above our heads just once before landing politely back on my hand. As soon as Ace is away from her, Maggie relaxes. "That was the scariest day of my life," she says.

"You and me both," I agree. "But it looks like Cadet Monroe has all the evidence he needs." Behind us, Cadet Monroe has Pashmina in handcuffs, and a satisfied grin on his face as he leads her away from the back gate. "Seems like he'll leave you alone now."

"My aunt and uncle will be thrilled," the Duke says. "The press is already talking about how Castle Atwood is setting a new standard for transparency." He glances over his shoulder at the crowd, where a group of reporters has gathered. Camera lights flash. "I think the positive press will help us make the case for saving the castle."

"Oh my gosh!" Maggie says, throwing a hand to her mouth like she's just remembered something. "I have to get ahead of the PR. This is too big. You two stay— I'll just— I'll be in the castle offices. Meet me there?" She doesn't wait for an answer before she scampers off, her phone already lighting up with messages.

"It seems I owe you a thank you yet again," The Duke steps forward and reaches out for my hand. He kisses the top of it, letting his lips brush over my skin ever so softly. "First you save my life. Then the castle. I suppose it was my lucky day when Maggie hired you."

Over the Duke's shoulder, I hear a throat clearing. The Duke steps aside, revealing Travis. He stares at the Duke and me, concern etched across his features.

"I heard the noise," Travis says stupidly. "I wanted to make sure you were okay."

"I'll leave you to it," The Duke nods at him before turning back to me. "But, Rebecca," he pauses, a gentle look in his eye. "I do hope you'll let me thank you with that dinner."

With that, the Duke leaves in the same direction Maggie went, no doubt eager to work with her to get ahead of the press. Travis stares at me like he's never seen me before.

"You solved a murder?" He says. "And the Duke— are you two—"

"Travis," I say, shaking my head. "I've thought about what you asked me. About a second chance."

Travis inhales sharply, looking at the ground as if he already knows what I'm going to say.

"And the thing is..." I tell him. "You broke something between us that mattered to me. And I had the courage to look at those pieces and try to rebuild something new for myself." I look around the grounds of Castle Atwood, marveling at how quickly they've become to feel like home. "I won't walk away from that now."

"Why?" Travis says, his voice sounding strained and desperate.

"Because I know what I deserve," I tell him.

With that, I turn on my heel and even though I expect to feel the urge to look over my shoulder, I don't. Instead, I hold my arm up in the air and whistle at Ace, who takes off in flight, heading straight back toward his perch in the atrium. Once his wings have disappeared into the safety of the barn, I lock the doors behind him.

Joe follows me, stuck to my heel like a shadow, and the two of us make our way across the courtyard. We head toward the open doors of Castle Atwood, where we know good food and friends will be waiting for us.

We stop at the steps that lead up to the castle's main entrance, its enormous doors beckoning us onward. I glance down at Joe. "What do you think, buddy? Are we home?"

Joe nudges my leg with his nose to urge me forward, and I know it's because he's hoping to wrangle a few snacks out of Chef before the evening is over.

Together, we head into the castle to look for Maggie and the Duke, knowing what's in front of us is better than what we've left behind.

CHAPTER

Thirty-One

A COUPLE OF DAYS LATER, Joe and I are walking around the village of Atwood with Maggie. She's making a special trip into town to buy more spiced honey for Chef Renauld, who uses it to craft her honey-flavored ice cream.

"I'll do anything to make sure I get my favorite dessert," Maggie says, stopping to examine a collection of scarves being sold at a nearby open-air market. "I should get the honey before something else takes my attention," she says, dropping the gossamer scarf back on the table in front of her. Her eyes scan the scarf wistfully, but she lets it rest on the table anyway. "I'll meet you guys back here in an hour?"

"Sounds like a plan," I tell her, enjoying the thought of an easy day spent wandering through the market place. Maggie waves goodbye as she disappears around a corner, and Joe and I weave our way through the shops together. He pants under the warm Mediterranean sun, his enormous tail wagging back and forth as it occasionally bumps my leg. We stop at various stands in the marketplace, inhaling the sweet scent of dried peaches and Monrovian plums.

When we reach the end of the marketplace, we pause at the newsstand. The shelves are littered with gossip magazines. It occurs to me I haven't seen the latest news on the castle. Last time I checked, we were "the Castle of Death." But maybe, since the open house, the coverage has changed.

I grab a magazine off the shelf and flip to the centerfold. The newsstand owner, Rodrigo, smiles at me. He's a middle-aged man with a plump belly and a grizzled beard. From what I've heard from the castle staff, he's a frequent informant for gossip magazines and is always looking for the next scoop. He's been known to interrogate castle staff on more than one occasion and even slip them some cash in exchange for information.

"Like what you see?" Rodrigo asks, a cheeky edge to his voice.

My eyes scan the centerfold, and I can't help but gasp at what I see. There's a picture of me standing next to the Duke at the open house, the castle framed in close-up behind us, hundreds of people milling about at the event. The article's title reads: "Animal Trainer Saves Monrovia Castle at Celebrated Public Open House: Who is Rebecca Orange?"

I blink my eyes open and shut, shocked to have made the news. Beside me, Joe lets out a bark as if he wants to see the picture. I bend down, showing him the image in the magazine. He nudges the corner with his nose, drawing my attention to something I hadn't noticed before: Joe's made the photo as well. He's by my feet in the picture, looking every bit like the movie star he is.

"Well," Rodrigo says, clearing his throat. "What do you think?"

"I think," I smile at him. "That this is just the start of a very big adventure."

———

Keep reading for an excerpt from "A Victim in the Village," Book Two in the Rebecca Orange Castle Cozy Mystery Series!

A Victim in the Village

CHAPTER ONE

"You're going to love this," Maggie says, taking my hand as she pulls me through the Village of Atwood. "All the vendors for the Foundation Festival will be there, and we get to be the first to sample what they're bringing to the festival!"

We round a corner, revealing a quaint street bordered by pastel buildings. Brightly colored flowers vine their way up the stucco walls. The sweet scent of honeysuckle fills the air. I've only lived in Monrovia for a few months, but already, it feels like home. The country is small and I haven't had a chance to see much of it, but the Village of Atwood is a jewel in its crown. Beside me, my giant Tibetan Mastiff-- Joe-- struggles to keep up, panting a little at the brisk pace we're keeping.

"I think Joe's been indulging a little too much in the snacks here," I tell Maggie. "He's gained about ten pounds since we moved to Monrovia."

Maggie waves a hand in the air as if numbers don't matter. "What's ten extra pounds when you already weigh over two-hundred?" She says brightly. "He looks great to me. Very handsome." We pass the fountain that serves as the center of the town square, the sound of the flowing water creating a peaceful ambiance in the village. Among the apartments that circle the courtyard, windows are closed and curtains are drawn. Almost everyone is asleep this early. We've come with a purpose, and we're beating the crowds.

"So what exactly did the Duke want us to do?" I ask, my stomach flipping a little at the mention of Jack— the Duke of Atwood— who also happens to be my employer. And who happens to be very charming. And attractive. And one of my favorite people to spend time around since we solved a murder together just a few weeks ago.

"The Foundation Festival is a big deal for the village," Maggie says, taking on the tone she uses when she's about to give me a history lesson. Due to the fact I'm still learning about my new home, I get these lessons a lot.

Maggie stops and points at a statue that stands on the street corner. It's marble, and features a beautiful woman in robes holding a basket of fruit. "Legend has it that Monrovia was founded by a woman," Maggie continues, pointing at the statue. "She was the leader of her tribe, and even in times of drought, she always made sure her people never went hungry. Her name was Monrosha, and she's the reason Monrovia exists today. The Foundation festival celebrates the history of our country, which is, I can proudly say, very female."

I stare up at Monrosha's face. Her cheekbones are high, her eyes closed. There's a determined expression etched into her features.

"That's a history to be proud of," I tell her.

"And as you can see, it's also history has to do with food!" Maggie points at the basket in the marble statue's hands, emphasizing the fruit within.

"Oh, that's why we both eat so much," I laugh. "It's not because we're gluttonus! It's because we're patriotic."

"Exactly," Maggie agrees. "Long story short, the Duke

wants us to taste test all of the vendor offerings that will be at the festival! And by the Duke... I mean me."

Maggie links her arm in mine. We continue walking down the cobblestone alley, making at turn onto a narrow road. "He said I could bring anyone I wanted, and I chose you."

"When you said we'd be going for an early breakfast, I had no idea it would be such an adventure," I tell her. We stop at our destination— Cafe de Flore— one of my favorite places to eat in Monrovia. It's part cafe, part bookshop, and the space features flowers throughout.

"Hey, when you're my friend, there's nothing but adventure!" Maggie says. She pushes open the front door. Joe follows her, and the three of us make our way into the familiar, book-lined storefront of Cafe de Flore. But we don't get very far before a bark escapes Joe's lips, followed by an emergency whine. It's a sound he's trained to use only when something is seriously wrong.

There, in the middle of the floor—

Is a body. A dead body.

Joe whimpers, running to hide behind me.

"You were saying about adventure?" I ask Maggie dryly.

She gasps, covering her mouth and taking a step back. "Not again," she says, shaking her head. "This can't be happening again."

I point at the slumped figured on the floor, a pool of blood gathering beneath his frame. "I think he would disagree."

———

To continue the adventure, order "A Victim in the Village," available now!

Lavender Latte Recipe

When Rebecca and Maggie visit *Cafe de Flore*, they always grab a lavender latte! You can make yours hot or iced. Just follow the recipe below:

Ingredients:

- 2 shots espresso or a regular cup of strong brewed coffee
- 8 oz milk
- 1 tbsp Torani Lavender Syrup
- 1 tbsp Torani Vannilla Syrup

Directions:

- Combine the coffee, milk, and syrup. Stir well.

- If serving iced, allow coffee to cool after brewing, then pour over ice with milk and syrup (the author's favorite).
- If you prefer, you can also substitute tea or decaf coffee.

More From Valerie Brandy

Available now in ebook and paperback:

The Private Investigator Annie Hudson Mystery Series:

- **Murder Behind the Gates — The Private Investigator Annie Hudson Mystery Series, Book One.**
- **"Murder in the Penthouse" — The Private Investigator Annie Hudson Mystery Series, Book Two.**
- **"Murder on the Farm" — The Private Investigator Annie Hudson Mystery Series, Book Three.**

The Predator / Prey Thriller Series:

- **"Trail of Obsession" — The Predator / Prey Thriller Series, Book One**
- **"Lies Run Deep" — The Predator/ Prey Thriller Series, Book Two**
- **"The Trap is Set" — The Predator / Prey Thriller Series, Book Three**
- **"The Woman in the Wind" — The Predator / Prey Thriller Series, Book Four**

<h1 style="text-align:center">Letter From the Author</h1>

Dear Reader,

Thank you for dedicating your time to the world of Monrovia and Rebecca Orange! These books mean so much to me, and my hope is always that what I've written gives you the chance to escape to a cozy new place.

I love hearing from readers (seriously, it makes the job so fun!). So I hope you'll visit me at www.valeriebrandy.com or find me on social media , even if it's just to say "hi" or talk about flower names for coffees. Monrovia is special because of the community there, and I love forming the same cozy friendships around my books.

You can also join my author club mailing list for free give-aways and updates on new releases.

Warmly,

— Valerie Brandy

www.ingramcontent.com/pod-product-compliance
Lightning Source LLC
Chambersburg PA
CBHW060417310726
48976CB00003B/1088